Smoke Screen Secret

MARIANNE HERING

Chariot VICTOR
PUBLISHING
A DIVISION OF COOK COMMUNICATIONS

DEDICATED TO:

Katie, Heather, Michelle, Jesse,
Emily, Lindey, and Samantha

Special thanks to Scott C. Swenka of Phoenix,
Arizona, for his pyrotechnical assistance. Any technical errors or omissions are deliberate so that no
copycat fires can be set using the information in this
book. Any other errors introduced in this book are
my mistakes or oversights, and for those I apologize.
MKH

Chariot Books is an imprint of ChariotVictor Publishing
Cook Communications, Colorado Springs, CO 80918
Cook Communications, Paris, Ontario
Kingsway Communications, Eastbourne, England

SMOKE SCREEN SECRET
© 1997 by Marianne K. Hering

Cover design by Scott Rattray and Andrea Boven
Cover illustration by Bill Silvers
First printing, 1997
Printed in the United States of America
01 00 99 98 97   5 4 3 2

One

Everyone knows that a kiss doesn't count if the guy has to do it for a play. But my friend Tasha didn't believe me. She said a kiss is a kiss is a kiss. I said, "It has to mean something."

"Oh, McKenna," she said, "it's like at Christmastime, when you get one underneath the mistletoe. Don't be so picky."

Tasha liked to keep track of how many guys she had kissed. I'd say a kiss underneath the mistletoe counted, but definitely not a kiss in a play. It had absolutely no romance because you got a grade for it. How can a real kiss be graded? Since we both went to the Palos Verdes School of the Performing Arts and were in lots of productions, it was an important rule.

"Will you guys stop arguing?" said my twin sister, Jade. "Someone is listening." She waved her head toward the school secretary, who was typing away in the office.

"So let her hear," I said. "If she doesn't have anything better to do than eavesdrop, then who cares?"

"I care," Tasha said. "I have to hang out here every day. I don't want Ms. Hancock hearing about my love life. Let's finish this at lunch."

"Finish what? This discussion is an absolute waste," Jade said, tucking her brown hair behind her ear. "I've never been kissed, and you don't see me in a panic to get one."

I had never been kissed either. But I would never say so out loud—especially not in front of tall, exotic-looking Tash, who had probably given her first kiss at about the same time I first gave a guy a black eye—in kindergarten.

My sister was too busy panicking about our upcoming general interview with a casting director to worry about anything else, let alone boys. She and I were seated in the reception area of the school office, waiting to talk with the principal about auditioning for a role in the remake of *The Wizard of Oz*. Tasha Kim, Jade's best friend, was there because she was an office aide that period.

Tasha said, "Speaking of kissing off, McKenna, look who's coming."

It was Ryan Kennett. My ex-almost-boyfriend. We liked each other last summer, but broke up before we ever got to the kissing part.

Ryan strolled through the door ahead of a burly hall monitor. Tasha said hi, and so did Jade. I never knew what to say to Ryan anymore, so I just sat there on the bench, silent.

"Hi, Jade. Hi, Tash," he said. "And since McKenna is not speaking to me, say hi to her for me."

"I am too talking to you," I said. "What did I do now?"

The hall monitor, a big man with a crew cut, put a hand on Ryan's back. "We don't have time to discuss any lovers' quarrels. We've got an appointment with the vice principal." He pushed Ryan out of the reception area.

I watched Ryan's wavy brown hair and blue jeans move down the long hall. He was holding his hand in an awkward position, pulled in close to his stomach.

The hall monitor deposited him on a hard, wooden bench outside the vice principal's office. No one ever wanted to see the vice principal, Mr. Harley. He was nothing but torture. Mr. Harley meant detention, intimidation, or expulsion. Probably all three. Besides that, Mr. Harley spits when he yells. I didn't envy Ryan. He'd get a minimum of at least three sprays, no matter what he'd done.

As soon as the hall monitor left, Ryan leaned forward and called in a whisper, "McKenna! Come 'ere."

At first I sat still, ignoring him. The school secretary, sitting behind her desk fortress, looked up and scowled. She went back to typing. I couldn't go, even if I had wanted to. Not with her watching me.

"What's the matter, McKenna?" Tasha said. "Are you really not even speaking to him? That's bitterly harsh."

As if on cue, the secretary stood and went into the faculty lounge, closing the door behind her. Now I had no excuse.

"Go on," Jade said. "He's practically on death row if he has to see Mr. Harley. Find out what he wants."

Ten seconds later, I stood facing him, my back to the reception area. I found out that Ryan wanted a favor. A secret favor.

"Why didn't you ask Tasha, your good friend?" I said, reminding him of the reason we argued last summer and I had decided not to trust him.

"Everyone knows she can't keep her mouth shut—" Ryan couldn't finish, because Mr. Harley's door opened, and he stood there, staring at us. His dark eyes reminded me of a hawk's, flicking here and there, looking for

something to swoop on and kill.

"Thanks for giving me that English assignment, McKenna." Ryan made up the excuse for Mr. Harley's ears. "Thanks." He grabbed one of my hands with both of his as if to shake it in gratitude and palmed off something.

After he walked into Mr. Harley's office, and the heavy door shut tight, I looked at what Ryan had given me. In my hand was a dead, white mouse.

*****

As I dangled him by the tail, his tiny front legs were curved like a coat hanger hook. The furry rib cage that should have been lifting and sinking was still. The rodent's eyes, glassy and red, had sunk in with death.

What am I supposed to do with this?

First I had to hide it, because if Jade or Tasha saw it, they would freak. Then Ryan would get in trouble for sure. I bet he had taken the mouse from the science lab.

I untucked my blouse and put my hand holding the mouse underneath. I saw a trash can near the photocopy machine. Once I got to the end of the hall, I would have about seven steps till I could throw the mouse away. No one would notice if I tossed him.

Several voices entered the office, asking Tasha questions and quietly chatting in the reception area.

Good. A distraction. No one will notice me now.

I was five steps away from the can. Four. Three.

"McKenna."

At the sound of the principal's voice, I jerked around.

In my heart I was expecting him to say, "Why are you smuggling dead rodents underneath your blouse? Didn't your mother ever teach you any better? If you're

hungry, wait for lunch like the rest of us."

Instead he said, "I'd like to introduce you to a casting director, Ms. Candy Cane."

At any other time, I would have laughed at such a name. But right then, all I really heard was "casting director." Since our acting school was only an hour's drive from many major movie studios, casting directors roamed the halls on a regular basis.

And casting directors recommend actors to be in movies.

I was an actor. I wanted a part in a movie. Thoughts of mice, dead or alive, scurried from my mind.

Miss Candy Cane, dressed in bright clothes and with a red lipstick smile painted on her mouth, walked straight toward me.

"I've already met your sister," Candy said. "I'm delighted to meet you." Like her name, Candy was bright and agreeable. A happy, friendly person.

She extended her right arm for a handshake. My arm instinctively slipped out from underneath my blouse. Then I stopped myself when I remembered the new pet.

"So," I said, dropping my hand to my side. "What agency do you represent?" I hoped she would forget the hand.

"Stars Unlimited," she said. She was nervous. I had thrown her off guard. But she didn't forget the shake. Probably thinking I was just a dumb kid and didn't know how to greet adults, she reached forward with both of hers.

I pretended I didn't see them.

"Oh, Stars Unlimited," I said, nodding my head with exaggerated friendliness. "That's great. What are you casting for today?"

"Children and teens for a remake of *The Wizard of Oz*," she said. "We're looking for a new Dorothy. A girl with a lot of genuine warmth and . . ."

She grabbed my hand suddenly. I couldn't jump. I couldn't move it away. I couldn't think.

As her five plump fingers encircled my hand, her warm palm pressed flat against fur.

We both felt the mouse move at the exact same instant, and our reactions were exactly the opposite.

I grabbed tighter.

She tried to yank her hand away.

I squeezed.

Candy squirmed.

"What are you doing?" she yelled. "Let me go!"

I did just as she asked, and poor mousey hit the cold, tile floor.

While I was looking down, my sister rushed over to my side and squatted to pick it up. "Oh, look! He's dead," she cried.

Then the little pest scampered out of her reach.

He's alive!

Tasha shrieked an ice-cube-down-your-shirt shriek.

Candy shrieked too. But for a different reason altogether. The mouse had just darted up her pant leg.

Two

Candy didn't stand around talking to me about Hollywood. In fact, she didn't stand around at all. She was too busy wriggling her body and snapping the elastic waistband of her slacks. The secretary escorted her to the restroom where she let the mouse go.

At least I hope she did, because I never saw it again. But I'll never know. With all those toilets around, Candy probably sent it to a watery grave.

As the people in the office began to leave, to go back to their classes or teachers' lounge, I wished for a million dollars. If I'd had it, I would have paid everyone in the room not to tell what had happened. But I didn't have a million dollars, and I watched the seven or so kids squeeze out the door, Tasha included, each racing to tell a bunch of friends about McKenna and the mouse.

Mr. Stanley should have just ended school that day, because no one learned anything. Who wanted to talk about the square root of one hundred twenty-one when they had me to talk about?

*****

Three periods later, Ryan Kennett met me in the hall.

"McKenna," he said, resting his arm on the top of my open locker, "I heard this geek telling a story about you. He said you put the mouse down a movie producer's shirt."

"That's not true!" I said. "It wasn't—"

"I knew it," he said. "I knew you'd never do something that stupid. Man, for a second there I was feeling pretty bad."

"Ryan, I never saw a movie producer. It was—"

"I mean, all you had to do was throw the mouse away after I gave it to you." He was talking himself out of any responsibility.

With both hands, I combed my fingers through my hair. I wanted to yank it out in frustration. This conversation was going nowhere.

"It was just a mouse from science lab," he said, "I gave it an overdose of—"

"Hey, Ryan," Tasha said, coming up behind us, "don't pick on McKenna. She doesn't want to talk about it. No girl in her right mind—"

"You guys! Listen!" I said, but they didn't hear me. I put my books inside my locker and got out some money for lunch.

Tasha's favorite mini-T and black leggings covered up her model-thin body. Since she was half Korean and half Russian, her face had an unusual bone structure. Even if she wasn't classically beautiful, no one ever passed her without looking twice. With the slight heel on her shoe, she was as tall as Ryan. They were literally talking over my head.

"You see," Tasha said, "McKenna thought the mouse was dead."

"Mouse?" Ryan said, pretending complete ignorance,

putting all the blame on me. "I thought it was a rat."

I slammed the locker shut. The bang made Ryan and Tasha jump.

As I walked away, I heard Ryan ask, "What's with her?"

Tasha said, "You know she's been moody ever since she got her first TV commercial. . . . Practically no one except us will be her friend."

*****

With a sister as good as Jade, I had an at-home best friend who went practically everywhere with me. Jade never did ask me why I shook hands with a mouse hidden in my palm. She never said, "You idiot. A casting director comes all the way to our school to meet us, and you shove a mouse in her hand." But I said it quietly to myself to make up for her silence.

"McKenna, don't worry about the mouse thing," she did say as we walked to the parking lot to wait for our ride home. "If God wants us to be in another movie, we'll be in a movie." She took hold of my wrist and said, "Remember this."

She was pointing out the matching ID bracelets we wore. Our names were etched on one side; the other side said, "Daughter of God." Mine was yellow gold, hers white.

A few cars passed by as we stood on the sidewalk on the lookout for Dad's car. Jade began walking back and forth, humming to herself. I began to pace. Pacing is the same thing as walking back and forth, except that walking means you're not in a hurry, and pacing means you are. I wanted away from school and the gossip.

Right as I paced past a gray garbage can, a body

leaped out from behind it and rolled in front of me. "Dive for cover!" it yelled. "Air raid!"

Even though I knew it was Ryan and he was joking, I looked up to check for bombers in the sky.

"Gotcha," he said, standing. "You thought it was real."

I tried to pretend I didn't care and walked away.

He followed. As he brushed some dried grass off his T-shirt, I wanted to reach up and pull some out of his dark hair, but it was impossible after this morning's mouse incident. I was never going to be nice to him again. Ignoring him was my plan.

"I know you're wondering what I was doing, even though you're ignoring me. I'm going to become a stuntman," he said, "and I need practice. I'm hanging around the parking lot so I can pretend I'm getting hit by cars. It really freaks the drivers out. I slam the hood with my elbow, yell, and then propel myself in front of the windshield. All they hear is a thud, and then they see this kid fly over their car. It's cool."

If I act all scared and tell him that's dangerous, he'll have to try it just to prove he can do it.

"Don't you think it would be more dramatic on the freeway?" I asked casually, since he'd already figured out I was trying to ignore him. To prove him wrong, I had to talk.

"Listen to you," he said. "Do I hear you telling me to go play on the freeway? McKenna, that isn't very nice. Especially since I'm probably one of the only people who'll still be your friend after that rat episode."

He had a point, even though he was to blame. My heart twinged just being reminded of that disaster, but I wasn't going to let him know I was worried about my school reputation, not to mention my career.

My twin, still humming and walking back and forth, headed toward us. "Jade," I called to her. When she looked my way, I said, "What do you suppose is keeping Dad so long? He's usually not this late on a Monday."

"But my mom is," Ryan said.

"So? What's that got to do with us?" I asked, searching his green eyes to find a clue.

"Didn't your dad tell you?" he said.

"Tell us what?" Jade asked, coming close.

"Oh, no," Ryan said. "I'm not the one who's going to tell you, especially McKenna. I thought that's the reason she wasn't speaking to me this morning. I know what you're going to do when you find out, and I don't want to be there. . . . I can't stand tears."

Three

Mrs. Kennett's station wagon finally pulled into the parking lot, and her son jumped on the rear bumper. He climbed on top of the roof and lay stomach-down, his face hanging in front of the windshield.

She rolled down her window, and I thought she was going to yell at Ryan, but she called to us, "Hey, girls!"

I walked over to see what she wanted.

"Hop in," she said. "Kennett taxi service awaits you."

"Did my dad ask you to pick us up?" I said, finally getting a clue as to what was going on.

"Didn't he tell you?" she asked. I inhaled her question with the exhaust from the car.

"Tell us what?" Jade joined in the conversation.

"Oh, no," she said, just as Ryan had. "I don't want to be the one. You ask him when he gets home."

I guess it was common knowledge that being the daughters of a doctor, we didn't spend a lot of time with our dad. Bummed because we hadn't seen him all weekend, I opened the rear door and threw my backpack inside, not too gently. Jade and Ryan climbed in on the other side.

"Hey, Mom," said Ryan. "Guess what McKenna learned at school today?" He looked at me and grinned. He was going to tell her the mouse story with me sit-

ting right there, listening to every word. If he hadn't been in the front seat, I would have been tempted to slug him in the arm.

"Oh," she said, "you mean about chasing the famous actress into the bathroom with a rat? I've already heard that story from the school secretary." Then she turned around and smiled at me. "But don't worry, McKenna. I didn't believe it. No one could be that stupid. And I didn't believe the part about her catching rabies, either."

I'd always wanted to be talked about for my great accomplishments, but not for something like this. I was going to be a social failure for sure.

*****

After our first TV commercial for cotton balls, my dad had gotten us an unlisted phone number because of all the crank calls. The best one was from an oil sheik who wanted to marry one of us in five years. Most of the calls, however, were from girls our age wanting to know how to get into the TV business. Some were from boys at our school who left weird messages. A couple of them were in bad taste, so Dad started screening the calls. But it was just too many. With the new phone number, the calls had stopped.

When we got home, Jade and I raced to the answering machine. We always did, even though we had left our school friends an hour or so ago.

The tape played a teen boy's voice, "Hickory, dickory, dock, the mouse ran up the pants!" The laughter in the background was worse than the butchered nursery rhyme. It meant five or six guys from my school were in on the joke, instead of just one. The tape machine was flashing a five, and I didn't want to hear four more mes-

sages like that. I went to my bedroom, leaving Jade to screen the rest.

When she came to find me lying on the bed, she was prancing with happiness. "You look as if you just had your first bite of a Snickers bar," I said. "What is it?"

"Our agent called," she said. "We've got an audition Saturday! Can you believe it? It's for a movie called *Thoroughbred Fever.* We'd get to work with horses!"

If it had been anyone else except Jade, I would have thought she was lying.

"Are you sure it wasn't Ryan or someone playing a joke?" I said. This was too weird to be true. It had been more than a month since our agent called. The only thing we were qualified for was *The Wizard of Oz.* And that dream was over. Finished. Dead.

"Tasha told me about *Thoroughbred Fever* only last week," she said. "It's the new project of actor/director Rand Knighton. His last film project won *three* Academy Awards."

"Is it a PG movie?" I asked, sitting up. "Dad won't let us be in anything with sex in it."

"I think so," said Jade. "Mr. Samuels knows Dad's rules. He said it was a 'family' movie."

"Jade," I said, "the last movie we were in needed twins. What if we audition and they only want one of us?"

"That hasn't happened yet. Don't worry about it."

"I won't," I lied.

Just as she was about to leave, I asked, "Did you give our phone number to anyone new?"

"I don't think so," my sister said. "I only give it out to five or six close friends."

"Then how did all those crank callers get it?"

*****

Dad came home after dinner. When I heard the garage door opening, I ran to the kitchen where the garage connected to the house.

Jade was already at the kitchen table, doing science homework. "Are you going to ask him," she said, "or should I?"

Before I could answer, he came through the door, looking like his usual self. Same boring black-rimmed glasses and short, dark hair. His arms were loaded with a briefcase, a plastic cooler, and *Time* magazine.

"Hi, girls," he said while carefully navigating around table and chairs to put his load on the tile counter. "Did you get the mail?"

Jade pointed to a pile of unopened envelopes and flyers on the table next to her books. From what I could tell, it was all bills and junk mail. Not very exciting stuff.

"Dad—" I began.

"Not now," he said; "you know I like to concentrate on the mail."

Dad was a careful reader. I couldn't wait for him to go through any bills, so I sat down next to Jade and started reading her science book.

"McKenna," he said, glancing my way, "what are you reading?" The plan worked. It must have taken him by surprise to see me doing homework. He always praised me when I did school stuff. He'd learned about positive reinforcement early on in college.

"Umm, it's about . . . ," I didn't know. I checked to make sure I was reading the book right-side up.

"Oxygen," Jade said, saving me. "We're studying the life cycle in class."

"You mean how mammals consume oxygen and expel carbon dioxide, while plants use the carbon dioxide in photosynthesis and make more oxygen?" Dad

19

said, loosening his tie.

"Exactly," my twin said. "Plants even absorb air pollution."

"There's a neat, simple science experiment to prove how valuable plants are to the oxygen chain," Dad said with enthusiasm. "You take one plant, two mice, and two airtight containers—"

I couldn't stand talking about mice. I interrupted him. "How come you didn't tell us Mrs. Kennett was going to pick us up from school?"

"Well," he said, "I thought she would have told you the good news."

"What good news?" Jade said. Even she was impatient now.

"That I've hired her as your personal manager," he said. "She's your legal guardian and can take you to auditions, rehearsals, and all of that." We weren't exactly cheering, so he added, "Plus she knows what to do. She's been taking Ryan and the other boys around—"

Jade lifted her book in front of her face. But I could still see her lower lip trembling. Ryan had been right— this was something to cry about. We never saw Dad on school nights or weekends, but he had always been there for us when we needed him for our career. Now he'd given that up, too.

"Also," he said, wanting to get it all over with, "I'm not going to be able to pick you up or take you to school anymore. Business is up now that everyone is coming in for the new surgery to get rid of forehead wrinkles. We just go inside and snip the nerves that help make the forehead move . . ."

What? Will I need plastic surgery to see my own dad now? And Mrs. Kennett? Why her? I was trying to ignore Ryan, and this little change of events makes me practically his sister. What else could go wrong?

20

Four

The coffee table, magazines, and receptionist behind a small window with a sliding glass pane made Galaxy Studios' reception area look like a dentist's office. Jade and I sat on the flowered, chintz sofa waiting for our turn to audition. I hoped it wouldn't be as painful as having a cavity filled.

"Don't worry, Jade," I said. "I won't blow this audition. I won't ask any questions about her facial hair."

"Why would you ask about her facial hair?"

"Didn't you see her when she called in that redheaded girl?"

"I didn't really pay attention," she said. "I'm trying to get psyched up. I'm concentrating on being unique, but natural. The first five seconds are often the most important."

She really takes those acting classes at school seriously.

"Well, her upper lip looks like Gracie's, if you ask me," I said.

Mrs. Gracie had been our baby-sitter when we were about ten. The doctor gave her some sort of hormone to help her have a baby. But before she grew big with a baby, she grew a mustache. I'd seen her use wax goop to peel off the hairs. Actually, it was kind of cute. The

21

chapped mark on her upper lip made it look as if she had just finished a glass of red punch.

I found myself smiling at the memory and relaxing.

"What about the veins?" I said to Jade after a few seconds of silence. "She's wearing really dark panty hose. Do you think she's covering up blue blood vessels? Should I give her Dad's number so he can do laser surgery?"

Before Jade could answer, a girl who was about two years older than we were, snickered. Sitting on the love seat opposite the receptionist, she hid her pert nose and blond hair behind a copy of *The Hollywood Drama-logue*. Her hand went up to cover her mouth.

Slap! A well-dressed woman sitting in a nearby wooden chair hit the girl's leg with a rolled-up glamour magazine.

"Ashley Dawn," the woman said, "don't bite your nails. It isn't becoming to a star."

I whispered to Jade, "Neither is scolding your daughter in public."

Then the receptionist called through the window.

"McKenna James, Ms. Haveshire will see you now."

Jade put her arm around me and gave a hug. "It'll be OK," she whispered. "Remember, if God wants one of us to get this role, nothing will stop Him." She twirled the bracelet on my wrist.

As I pushed through the swinging doors, I wondered why God wanted us to be in Hollywood. A friend of mine had once asked me to memorize a line from the Bible, and I thought of it then: "I am sending you out like sheep among wolves. Therefore be as shrewd as snakes and as innocent as doves." I always tried to remember that being famous and rich weren't the most important things in acting. Since I loved God, finding

out what was right to do in His eyes and stopping evil were more important. And this business, I was learning, was full of people who acted like wolves.

Ms. Haveshire met me in the hallway. She let me soak in the framed photos of movie stars, which all had "To Marti, With Love, So-and-So" written on them. Ms. Haveshire certainly was proud of them. Even through her professional mask, she was beaming like a little kid showing you her pictures on the refrigerator. I hoped my photo would be up in her hallway one day.

When I was done examining the glossy collection, she extended her palm.

This time I didn't have a mouse, and I shook the small hand with five neat, clean fingernails, trying not to stare at the rash on her lip. *Her hands are definitely not wolflike,* I thought. *Her hands are as delicate as a bird's wing.*

"It's always a pleasure to do casting for Rand Knighton," she said after we dropped hands. "I recommended Rand to be cast in his first movie role. As soon as he became a director, he hired me to cast all his productions. He almost always takes my first recommendation." She deliberately caught my eye.

Since personality power and charisma were key in the movie business, I looked directly into her gray eyes and smiled, oozing self-confidence. She gazed right back into my green eyes for a long time, as if she had X-ray vision.

Because I'm an identical twin, I've learned to let people stare at me. Ms. Haveshire took her time trying to find some mark, some bend in the nose or a lift of an eyebrow that distinguished me from Jade.

I studied her, too. Her hair was as black as her suit, too black to be natural. Her face was pale with light-

colored lips, and she wore eye shadow that would pass for the dust of burnt charcoal. When she turned to lead me through a double door, the smirk on her face told me she thought she could tell me apart from my sister.

But I knew that if she met me on the street tomorrow, she'd be floundering for the right name. Jade and I looked *exactly* alike. Only my dad never got us confused.

"Please," Ms. Haveshire said, showing me the room, "make yourself comfortable."

I nodded, sensing that she wouldn't like me to be chatty, and looked around. A few metal folding chairs were set up in no particular order. Three video cameras, a potted plant, and a row of five men were in the room. Not one man said anything, and they had to try hard to look that mean. It was like going into the bathroom at school and finding a group of older girls smoking. They would never talk to me, but their eyes said, "We're too cool for a little twit like you."

Ms. Haveshire sat on the edge of a plain black desk and picked up a manila folder. She glanced up and down at the photograph and papers my agent had delivered to her.

"I see you're a beginner," she said without looking up.

Though I had been a model basically since birth, my list of acting experience was short, but strong.

One TV commercial for Swan Softie cotton balls had qualified me for the Screen Actors Guild, or SAG, as the industry called it. The membership made me eligible to audition for movie roles that had been closed to me only a few short months ago. Any of the kids in my acting classes would joyfully swap their credit cards for a SAG card and the experience it represented.

Last summer I had acted in a movie produced by a midsized company. Since then, I'd done three more Swan Softie ads. For a teen, I was no beginner, and from the look in her eye, she knew it too.

Everyone in this room is trying to make me nervous, but not one is going to get to me.

After she asked me a few questions about school and why I wanted to be an actor, she stood up. "Let's hear you read for the part," Ms. Haveshire said, her voice controlled and strong. "I'll be Aunt Savannah. You are Cassidy."

I picked up the script for *Thoroughbred Fever* that she slid across the desk with her index finger. I flipped through the pages. My character was supposed to confront her aunt who had been stealing and selling family heirlooms to support her failing horse-racing business.

The hard part would be showing anger without looking ugly. If I got too emotional, my face would turn red. No audience wants to see a kid with a blotchy face.

"OK," Ms. Haveshire said. "I'll sit behind the camera over there. Pretend that potted plant is Aunt Savannah. I need you to walk into the scene, then stop on a two shot with the plant. You know what to do with the tape marks on the floor?"

I did. I nodded and walked to the far corner of the room where I was to begin. My on-camera classes at school had drilled into my brain how and where to walk in front of a camera. I knew the tape marks were to tell me where to stop and turn. And I knew never to look directly at the camera.

A guy in jeans and a black shirt got behind the camera. Another flipped on two spotlights. The others picked up clipboards to take notes. One held up a black-and-white clapboard with my name on it in front of a

camera. As he closed it, he said, "Rolling." A little red light on the camera came on.

Ms. Haveshire read her part in a monotone voice. "Well, I see you've been snooping around the stables again, Cassidy." She hardly looked at the script, but watched me the whole time.

If she knows the part so well, she must have auditioned a lot of people.

"Yes," I said, "and I've been snooping in the attic as well. Where are all the paintings of our family's winning horses?" I hoped a defiant tone was right. If I ever talked that way to my dad, I'd be in my room in five seconds, on restriction for life.

I think I guessed right. I saw Ms. Haveshire's eyebrow shoot up, and she put a little more into Aunt Savannah's reading.

"Are you threatening me?" she asked like the Wicked Witch of the West.

"No," I said, "I just want the paintings. To me, they are worth more than money because they're part of our family history, and Grandfather feels the same. I think I'll talk to him about them—today!"

At the end, I knew I had clinched it. In the last scene, Cassidy had to cry. I rarely cry. But there is one thing that will always get to me. I think about how much I miss my dead mother, and the tears that stream down my face are real. It seems kind of dishonest in a way, but it's what gets the job done. I know she would be proud of me.

I hoped Ms. Haveshire was.

Five

Jade had her audition right after mine. And as soon as she finished and stepped back into the waiting area, the receptionist called for Ashley Dawn.

The blond was almost too perfect. With the silky hair grown past her waist, the upturned nose, and a pair of pink pursed lips, she looked like a Barbie doll gone Beverly Hills.

"Now remember, Ashley," the woman said while fiddling with her daughter's hair, "don't blow this. I can do everything else for you, but you've got to get this part. Visualize yourself on the big screen. Be in harmony with the ideas and words . . ."

"Don't worry, Mother," Ashley said, fluffing the hair her mother had just pushed back. "I'm perfect for the part. And I've worked myself into Ms. Haveshire's good graces." She fumbled in her purse for some lipstick and glided it on. She blotted her lips on a tissue, made a kissing sound in the air, and strolled through the swinging doors.

"Don't forget to project!" Ashley's mom called. Then she took a cigarette out of a gleaming gold case. As she lit the cigarette with an equally shiny lighter, I started to cough in protest.

"McKenna," Jade said. "Just ignore the smoke. Dad will be here any minute to pick us up."

"No, he won't," I said and coughed again. "He's probably golfing."

"He said he would be back in one hour," she countered. "He's only three minutes late, and he was going to the health food store a few blocks from here. He's not golfing."

"Is there a golf course within ten miles of this place?" I asked.

"I think there's one near the foothills—"

"Then he's golfing," I said. "Why else did he put golf clubs in the trunk of the car? Face it, he's a plastic surgeon, and all doctors are addicted to golf."

Not wanting to argue within earshot of Ashley's mom, I changed the subject. "How did your audition go?" I sensed rather than saw Ashley's mom sit up in her chair to listen.

"Wasn't that a great role?" Jade said. "I know I did well at the end when Cassidy cries, but the first anger scene . . . I just don't think it's that—"

"Excuse me, girls," Ashley's mom said. "But aren't you the twins who filmed *Clone Colony?* I recognize you from the newspaper photos."

"Yes," I said and coughed again as if dying of pneumonia. I pushed the ashtray on the coffee table toward the woman, challenging her to put the cigarette out. Slowly she snuffed the cigarette, grinding it into the brass container with three twists of her wrist.

"Nasty business with those drug smugglers?" the woman said in a way that begged for more information. She looked at Jade with one plucked eyebrow raised, expecting the whole story as payment for snuffing the cigarette.

"It wasn't fun," my sister said. "But the newspapers weren't lying. The director filmed the producer and some crew members loading cocaine onto a boat. They were arrested. The whole movie almost fell apart, but we finally finished."*

"Who is your agent?" the woman asked. "She must be good to have gotten *you* two a movie role."

Knowing I would take the comment as an insult, Jade answered with her best manners, "Barnaby Samuels Agency, Mrs. . . . I don't believe we've been introduced."

"Alexis Saunders," she said. "Just call me Alexis. My daughter is Ashley Dawn."

I'd never heard of Ashley and never seen her before that day, and I guess my face showed it.

"You know," Alexis said, coaching us, "she plays on a soap opera called *Seems Like Eternity.*"

"Gee, Mrs. Saunders," I said, "I guess we missed her. We were probably wrapped up in filming a motion picture or something. Otherwise I'm sure we would have seen her on TV."

With her foot, Jade pressed down on mine, which was underneath the coffee table. She was trying to stop a fight. But this woman was too snobby. She had to be stopped.

"Mrs. Saunders?" I continued, despite a jab in the ribs from Jade. "I'm curious . . . why did you want Ashley to project? That's for stage acting. With the camera, you don't worry about stuff like that. Is this some new technique . . . or is Ashley a beginner?"

Alexis Saunders breathed four times deeply, as if she were exhaling during an aerobics workout. Then she reached for her cigarette case again.

I looked at Jade's face. Her eyes were closed, and I

bet she was praying. I probably had gone too far, but something about this woman bugged me.

I bet Jade prayed that Dad would come quickly, because he walked through the door. I relaxed, glad that we could leave.

"Dad!" I said, jumping up from the couch. "Let's go. Can we get something to eat? I'm starved."

"OK," he said. "So you worked up an appetite? That's good. This morning you wouldn't eat a thing."

Jade stood to join us and turned to the woman. "Mrs. Saunders," she said. "I hope Ashley's career goes well. I wish her luck on the soap opera."

And then the mood of the gathering turned as weird as garlic-flavored chewing gum.

"Saunders?" Dad said. "Ashley Saunders?" He peered through his thick-rimmed glasses at the woman lighting up a cigarette.

She looked at him and said slowly, deliberately, "I don't believe we've ever met."

But Dad didn't pick up on the hint that she didn't want to be recognized.

"Oh, yes, we have, Alexis," he said, smiling. "Does Ashley finally like her nose job? You didn't come back after the third revision. So I guess she liked it."

*This story is told in *Trouble Shooting*, Book One of the Lights, Camera, Action Mysteries.

Six

Three months later, Dad, Jade, and I were eating dinner together at home. It was a rare occurrence ever since Mrs. Kennett became our personal manager.

We had gone on several more auditions, but hadn't been offered a part in a movie, a commercial, or a bit part on a TV program.

Dad suddenly pushed away from the pasta and shrimp. "My pager's vibrating," he said and walked to pick up the phone.

I sat in a huff, arms crossed, and chewed my bottom lip. I looked at Jade and knew she was thinking the same thing: *We need a Dad who stays home every once in a while.*

"I can be at the emergency room in twenty-five minutes," Dad said. As he turned the phone off, he said, "There's been a car accident. I've got to go sew up someone's face. I'll help with the dishes when I come back."

I scooted my chair back and took my half-full plate to the kitchen. From the sink, I turned on the garbage disposal and said just loudly enough to be heard over the noise, "If he really wants to help, he can stay home for more than forty-five minutes."

I know I would have received a lecture, but the tele-

phone rang first.

I rushed to the eating area, beating Jade to the phone on the buffet where Dad had left it. It was Tasha.

"You guys!" I heard her squeal through the line. "Turn on the TV. Channel 4 News. Hurry."

*****

The smoke behind the newscaster was thick and black. It wafted out of the soundstage at Galaxy Studios. The huge roll-up door was open, and gray clouds misted out to the open air.

"... fire blazed for just a few minutes before firefighter Marcus Harris rescued actress Ashley Saunders from the dressing room. Four members of the crew and Saunders suffered from smoke inhalation. . . . Rand Knighton, the director, was not at the scene. . . ."

"There's that soap opera girl," I yelled at the TV. "She got my part in *Thoroughbred Fever*. She's playing Cassidy."

"Shhh—" Jade said. "Listen."

The camera panned to the crazed sound studio. In the background I could make out a woman who could have been Ms. Haveshire.

"... the cause of the fire has not yet been determined," the voice from the TV said.

Two men were putting Ashley onto a gurney. As the men lifted the portable bed into an ambulance, an attendant strapped an oxygen mask onto her face.

Dad, who had followed us into the den, said, "I'm leaving for the hospital. Call me if anything unusual happens."

*****

Two days later, Dad signed the contract for us to appear in *Thoroughbred Fever.*

Ashley Dawn was not coming back to the set. In fact, she was suing Galaxy Studios for "endangerment and psychological distress." Since state law and union rules prevented anyone under eighteen years old from working more than nine hours a day, and film crews worked an average of twelve, they wanted two actors. If they had both of us playing one role, they could speed up production.

Rand Knighton wanted both of us, Ms. Haveshire had said, because Galaxy Studios was behind on filming due to the fire. The role was ours now.

The only catch was we had to dye our hair.

*****

Even if it meant having more fun, Jade did not want a bleach job.

I had always wanted to do weird stuff to my hair, but Dad wouldn't allow it. So this was a dream come true for me, a nightmare for Jade.

Dad didn't understand girls' stuff. Even though he could afford to pay more, he usually only let us go to the cheap salons where you can't make an appointment. You have to wait for little kids to stop wiggling so the stylist doesn't lop off an ear, or for old men with crew cuts to get moving after the buzz is finished. At those places, you even have to pay extra for a blow-dry.

The studio was paying for this one, so Dad couldn't stop us from going to a fancy salon. And since we had to look exactly alike, we had the exact same stylist.

He began with Jade.

"It's going to take about five rinses to get it the exact color," Claude said, running his fingers through her hair. "It's a pity, really. Your hair is so silky and such a beautiful color. It reminds me of cherry cola."

Then Beatrice, the assistant, draped a smooth, soft apron around me. I settled in. For the rest of the afternoon, we sat in a Beverly Hills beauty salon and listened to Claude and Beatrice discuss our career, and everyone else's in Hollywood.

I felt weird in that big chair, staring into the mirror watching hands gob the color through. Part of me wanted to run because they both had bad dye jobs. He was fifty or so, and shoe-polish black hair sprouted from his head in thinned-out wisps. He wore it like a seventies' rock star's, long and combed back. Beatrice looked old enough to be in college, and her hair just missed being strawberry blond. Instead, it had just a tinge too much orange and had too much of a tease. It looked like cotton candy.

"Lucky for your sister—and you, McKenna," Claude said, rinsing the second batch of color out of my hair, "that Ashley Dawn got scared in that fire and quit. I guess she couldn't take the heat." He laughed at his own joke while rubbing my head with a towel. Next he pinned my hair up with a huge silver alligator clip. I wondered if his rings and diamond bracelet ever got damaged from the salon chemicals, or maybe they were fake and he didn't care.

"You two," he continued, "are so much better suited for Cassidy. I wonder what wild hare made Haveshire choose Ashley first. Anyone with half a brain can see that Jade—I mean, you two are, or will be—just perfect."

He went to Jade's chair to rinse her hair. "I've got to get this out before the hair falls out."

"Maybe Knighton chose Ashley because they are

both lousy tippers," muttered Beatrice, who was stirring more color glop into a bowl.

I made a mental note to make sure I left a tip. I hadn't known I needed to leave any since the studio was paying. I wondered if Jade knew and decided to leave extra, just in case she didn't. I didn't want to make Beatrice mad. Next time, she might turn my hair green on purpose.

"So when does production begin?" Claude asked after coming back from my twin's chair.

"Tomorrow," I said. "They're not even waiting for a formal costume fitting."

"Tomorrow!" he said. "Didn't you get hired just yesterday?"

"They've already rebuilt the part of the set that the fire destroyed," I said. "We can start tomorrow."

We both looked over at Jade. Hair wrapped up in aluminum foil, she was sitting across the room underneath a hair dryer. When she saw me, she waved. "Lucky for you, you're a twin," he said, "otherwise you might not have gotten the job."

I decided to ignore the insult. "No," I said, waving back to Jade. "I'm not just lucky. God has a reason for me to be in this movie."

"Well," Claude said, "you had better watch out when you're dealing with God." He bent down, his face next to mine. I could see spots on his face that weren't really moles or freckles. "I remember hearing about some twins when I went to Sunday school," he whispered.

"Jacob and Esau, they were called. God loved one more than the other."

"I've seen some directors who think they are gods," Beatrice added. "And Mr. Knighton is one of them. You'd better watch out, just as Claude says."

Seven

We were early for the first day of filming, and it was Mrs. Kennett's fault. When she came to pick us up, Jade was ready, but I still had to floss and change earrings.

"Jump in, girls," Mrs. Kennett said when we got to the car. "Let's step on it." I think she was more excited to meet the Hollywood people than we were. Her red hair was poufed and sprayed, and it looked good, considering she was a mom. She didn't say she was sorry for being twenty minutes ahead of schedule.

I stretched out in the backseat, but Jade rode up front. She didn't waste a second before she popped a cassette into the tape deck so we could rehearse our lines. Because of the rush to learn the part, we had taped the script, first with Cassidy's lines, then without. As soon as we had the lines memorized, we listened to the tape with only other people's lines to give ourselves a cue. That's how we studied. We played the cue tape over and over again until the script was as familiar as *Twinkle, Twinkle, Little Star.*

As we inched along the Hollywood freeway, Jade and I were repeating our lines together.

"Oh, no! Look! Thunderbolt has escaped!" we yelled, loud enough to get a few sideways glances from Mrs.

Kennett. But we didn't care. It was part of the script.

I felt a tap on my shoulder. My back contracted in shock. Slowly I turned.

Ryan.

He held his finger up to his lips, motioning me to be quiet. I nodded in agreement.

He ducked behind the seat again, hiding himself in the wagon part of the car. I looked back. All I could see was a body-sized lump underneath a UCLA stadium blanket. I grabbed my address book out of my backpack and tore out an empty page. I wrote, "What are you doing?"

Stretching my arm across the back of the seat, I casually dropped the note and pen behind it. They soon came sliding back over.

"My mom said I couldn't come," he had written, "but I didn't want to miss your first day. Do you think she'll kill me?"

"Yes," I wrote, and underlined it.

I had just finished dropping it back when Jade said, "McKenna, you've missed all your lines for scene six. Do you want me to rewind the tape?"

"Sure," I said, "that would be great."

As we sped down the freeway in the car pool lane, I noticed Mrs. Kennett was going over the speed limit by twenty miles per hour.

"Good luck, girls," Mrs. Kennett said. "I had counted on traffic being slow. As it is, we're going to be almost a half-hour earl—Ryan Henry Kennett!" She slammed on the brakes to slow the car. "What are you doing? You think you can hide from me and just walk right into that movie studio to watch? Did you think I wouldn't recognize my own son?"

Wearing a lopsided smile, he climbed over the seat

and sat next to me.

His mother eyed him in the rearview mirror. "When we get home, young man, you're going to catch it."

"Well, if you don't want me . . . ," he said, pulling on the door handle until it clicked, "I'll play on the freeway."

His joke went a little too far. Mrs. Kennett hit the door lock button on her control panel. She must have unlocked the doors because Ryan's flung open. A gust of air swooshed into the car, and he yelled, "See ya, Mom."

The car veered to the right as Mrs. Kennett turned around to see what was happening. A horn blared, and she swerved back into her lane.

Ryan lunged toward the open door. But instead of falling out, he grabbed for the door handle. At first he couldn't get the door to close. I leaned over and grabbed one of his arms and yanked. Together we had enough leverage to pull the door shut.

I don't know what Mrs. Kennett would have done had Jade and I not been there. But the look she gave Ryan made him sit up straight and fasten his seat belt.

His mom's face was so red it matched her hair. She opened her mouth to say something, but all she could do was suck in air and swallow. I think if she had tried to talk to Ryan, her voice would have growled like a forest beast's. She wisely remained quiet.

Besides rehearsing our lines, not another word was spoken until she listed our names for a guard sitting in a little gatehouse. After giving Mrs. Kennett directions to Stage 30 and checking our names off a list, he let us pass.

We came to the back lot. The studios looked like warehouses on the outside. On the inside, however, I

knew anything could happen. On the inside, ships sank, buildings exploded, babies were born, movies were made.

I didn't get a chance to knock on the door, which had a sign on it that said, "CLOSED SET—Cast and Crew Only," because a very small man in an olive-green jumpsuit pushed it open. I guessed he was a set carpenter or something because of the red toolbox he carried. He passed us on the cement stairs, lowering his head.

"Hey," Ryan said to the man, "can we just walk in?"

"Suit yourself," the carpenter mumbled through his mustached mouth, and then he walked down the stairs, two at a time.

The open door called to me. I peered into the studio. Because it was dark inside and bright outside, it took a few seconds for my eyes to adjust to the lighting. I entered without really knowing what I was getting into.

We walked down a hallway with doors on both sides. After we passed the wardrobe, makeup, and craft services entrances, we found the waiting room for actors, the talent lounge. Since no one was inside yet, we kept walking to the end of the hall. At the entrance to the sets was a sign that read, "Do not enter when light is flashing."

"The light is off," Ryan said. "I say we go in." Just as his hand touched the knob, a bell rang, and the red light turned on.

I covered my ears. So did Jade. We knew the noise and light were a warning that they were filming inside.

Ryan, however, hurled himself back down the hall, screaming, "Air raid!" He hit the indoor-outdoor carpet with a forward roll. Then he rolled sideways till he was "safe" underneath a door frame.

"Ryan," Mrs. Kennett called, "quit the stuntman

antics. As long as you're here, behave."

He dusted himself off, and all of us were silent as we waited for the light to turn off. Ryan met my glance and winked. Last summer, I would have smiled back. But I didn't want to let him think I was flirting, so I turned away.

When the light went off, we walked inside the double doors. As they closed behind us, I got goose bumps just thinking about doing a motion picture in such an old studio. I wondered what great actors and directors had made award-winning films inside these sound-proof walls. I wondered what I would learn here.

I had no idea that playing on the freeway would have been a lot safer.

Eight

"Wow," Ryan said. "They could take over the world from here."

Looking around, I understood what he meant.

From where we entered, we could see into the set of a luxurious living room. Above it hung enough equipment to build a satellite. Below the lights, the place was a human beehive. People were all over—moving cameras, hanging lights, hammering two-by-fours. The computers and boards for the sound equipment and cameras looked like equipment for a CIA investigation.

A bunch of leather director's chairs were set up near one corner, but they were empty. I doubted if anyone would sit down right then. The crew was too busy creating a world. The cameras and boxes of film and other equipment were on dollies, and the men pushing them looked as if they were carrying cargo ten times their weight.

I knew from working on *Clone Colony* how to find the director. He would be like the queen bee. Rand Knighton would be near a busy group, but no one would go near him. The rest of the bees created the colony. They would leave him alone to think, to look, to create in his head the scene they were about to film.

People would come and go, bringing the assistant director (AD) things for approval. Prop coordinators would hang a picture or move a table according to a diagram. Rand would have at least two ADs milling about, a director of photography (DP), and a key grip moving lights and cords. Everything on the set would be done, and then Mr. Knighton would consult with the DP. "Can I do the scene this way?" he would ask. Then, lights and camera tracks would be adjusted to make the new vision.

Jade grabbed my arm. "Look over there, McKenna," she said, pointing. "I think I saw a horse on the next set. Let's go see."

I followed her through the living room set into the next one.

There it was. A horse. A beautiful black beast. Every kid has met an animal like that at least once in a dream. It was the kind of horse you'd name Lightning or Midnight or Magic.

That must be Thunderbolt.

And it was inside a tiny set created to look like a horse stall. It nuzzled against a young man in jeans and a tank T-shirt who sat in the corner, fiddling with some straw.

I don't know how long my sister and I just stared at the horse, but before I knew it, Mrs. Kennett was at our side introducing a petite black woman named LaShondra as the talent coordinator.

"You're early," LaShondra said, smiling. "You're never supposed to come in here unless you've been called." She paused and then added, "Mr. Knighton can't stand that."

LaShondra had long, black, corkscrew-curled hair. Her attitude was so cheerful that when she told us we

were basically trespassing, it sounded like a compliment. She moved with a natural bounce, and the way she walked reminded me of a chipmunk.

"Where's Ryan?" Mrs. Kennett asked, so as not to let LaShondra hear.

I shrugged. I had been too busy looking at everything to notice he had vanished. Jade didn't even hear the question. She was too enchanted with the horse.

"I hope Ryan doesn't destroy the studio," Mrs. Kennett said under her breath.

LaShondra met us on the ramp. "I guess we'll find Ms. Haveshire first. Then you're off to makeup!"

We followed her back through the living room set. The walls were plywood with wallpaper. The fireplace wasn't much sturdier. I could have knocked a hole in the Styrofoam. It's hard to believe how little it takes to give the illusion of an entire solid house. With a little shove, I could knock down a whole wall.

Just as we were walking through the door, Mr. Knighton walked in. LaShondra stopped bouncing and began explaining. "Oh, I'm sorry, Mr. Knighton. We found the girls wandering . . . This is Mrs.—"

"Lorraine Kennett," she introduced herself.

If Rand Knighton was mad, then he hid it well. And when he shook Mrs. Kennett's hand, I thought he held it a little too long. But she didn't mind. I was glad Ryan wasn't there to see his mom acting like any junior high girl around a high school football player.

Sure he had thick, blond hair and great blue eyes. But he was ancient. At least forty. He could have been my dad. Maybe it was the money that had made Mrs. Kennett want to pouf her hair up that morning. His watch looked very expensive. His clothes, too, appeared casual, but you couldn't get quality like that at the mall.

Those clothes came from Beverly Hills shops—the kind where you need an appointment just to go inside.

"This is McKenna," Mrs. Kennett said, when she finally came to. She pushed me forward as if I were a five year old meeting a new teacher. "And this is Jade. Come on up, dear."

Putting one arm around each of us, he steered us toward the door. He took Mrs. Kennett's cue to treat us like kids and said, "You girls run along and go to make-up with LaShondra. Today we'll start filming with Jade, OK?"

I guess it had to be. He was the director.

*****

LaShondra took us to the makeup room. At the door, Mrs. Kennett excused herself to get a cup of coffee. But I knew she was really going in search of her son.

LaShondra pointed at Jade. "Sandra will do you up first today." To me she said, "I'll get you to the set schoolroom in a few minutes. But first, I have to check on some other actors."

Great, Jade gets to be with Thunderbolt, and I get to study.

"I think I'll just watch," I told LaShondra as she was leaving. I plopped down on a pink couch inside the small room with a posh interior. I wanted to make it look as if I were there to stay.

Sandra ran her hands through Jade's hair. "Claude did this job, didn't he?" she asked and plugged in a curling iron.

"Uh-huh."

"Are you going to stay blond after the movie?" Sandra draped a smock around my sister's shoulders. It

was identical to the one she wore.

"No!" Jade said.

"Why not?" Sandra said. "Even though Ashley's is natural, you two make better blonds than she does."

Right after Jade got a puff of powder, two TV newsmen came in. The call letters KKSC were written bright and big on the side of a long camera, which was saddled on one man's shoulder.

Whatever Rand Knighton did was news. If he had a hangnail, the whole world would know. So the first day of production after a fire would certainly bring reporters. Just saying his name on the five o'clock news instantly guaranteed viewers.

"I'm Ted Smith," the newscaster in navy said. "We're inside the production studio of Rand Knighton's *Thoroughbred Fever*. With us are the James sisters, McKenna and Jade, the replacements for Ashley Dawn Saunders, former star of the production." The newscaster shoved a microphone that looked like a sno-cone in Jade's face.

"How do you feel coming to this set after being on the troubled *Clone Colony* movie set?" The man asked. "Do you feel as if you're jumping from the frying pan into the fire?"

"No," she said, "Rand Knighton has everything under control. *Thoroughbred Fever* will be a success."

"Thanks, Miss James," said Ted. He turned to the cameraman. "Should we get a shot of the horse?"

"Sure," said the technician.

Sandra, used to such interruptions, picked up the curling iron and began to turn the ends of Jade's hair under.

"This stuff smells weird," Jade said.

Sandra picked up a round brush to fluff the curls and

put the hot iron down. It touched a hand towel lying on the counter. Suddenly, the terry cloth burst into an orange flame.

Jade instinctively tried to smother the fire with the end of her smock. The plastic-coated material began to burn up faster than a Kleenex in a furnace.

Nine

"Fire!" Sandra screamed.

"Drop!" I yelled, glad to remember instructions from kindergarten safety lessons. "Jade, drop and roll."

There was hardly any empty room on the carpeted floor. She fell down next to a chair. The first thing I grabbed was another towel. I threw it over her head so the fire wouldn't get to her hair.

Then, jumping on top of her, I wrapped my arms around her shoulders and rolled back and forth, hitting chair legs and cabinet doors.

The smoke smelled like a chemistry classroom.

We hadn't swayed more than a minute when I was hoisted off by a pair of strong arms. All I could see was a man's elbows and a short-sleeved blue shirt. Worried about my sister, I didn't think and kicked him in the shin to make him let me go.

He didn't even notice, but moved me, none too gently, off to the side.

"Jade, keep rolling," I yelled from where I had been pushed against the wall. But she didn't really need to. The flames were gone. The chemicals on the smock had all burned up.

The man turned Jade over onto her back. He was

checking to make sure she could breathe. While he pressed his thumbs into the side of her neck to check her pulse, the sprinklers finally came on.

Water washed away the smoke. The "rain" smelled of copper piping, and it mingled with the stench of melted plastic. Jade sat up with her head in her hands, sobbing, the water mixing with her tears.

*****

The movie studio and Mrs. Kennett had already sent flowers to Jade's hospital room by the time she finally got to rest. The bouquet from Galaxy Studios with its jungle plants was so big it could have been for a funeral. The one from Mrs. Kennett was a simple dozen yellow roses.

When Dad came, he brought a box of jelly beans. "I get the strawberry ones," I called.

"They're for Jade," he said. Turning to her, he said, "Let me see the shoulder."

Jade dutifully peeled away the hospital gown and showed him her right collarbone. Dad took off the gauze netting covering the burn. It was about the size of a grapefruit, red and shiny. A T-shirt with a regular collar would cover it, but nothing scoop-necked.

"Don't worry about those blisters, honey," he said, lifting her chin. "I golf with the best skin graft specialist in the state. We'll get this fixed up right." He looked at his watch. "I've got to catch your doctor before he goes on his next rounds. I want to check your charts."

After he left, I inspected the flowers. Jade was dividing up the jelly beans. She hated coconut and licorice ones. I was hoping she'd let me have at least a few of my favorites.

There was an envelope jammed in the middle of the

jungle flowers. It wasn't flat, so I could tell something besides a card was inside.

"Open this," I said.

She slid her thumb under the flap. Out slid a silver chain with a crystal pendant on it. She opened the card. "It says, 'There's mystical power in crystals. Galaxy Studios hopes it heals your burn and your soul.' " She looked happy for the first time since we left Thunderbolt.

"Can I see it?" She held the necklace out to me, and I took it. It didn't look mystical. It looked like a piece of rock candy, only more shiny. "This gives me the creeps. I don't think you should wear it."

"Why not? It's just a necklace."

"I don't like that stuff about 'mystical power,' " I said. "Remember, we aren't going to be superstitious anymore. We—and especially you—decided that prayer is the best thing for getting help. There is God, you know."

"But what if He made the rock to have special power?" She reached out for the crystal. "What if God made it for good?"

"Well . . . it just seems weird, as if we're going backward."

"Oh, McKenna, you're probably just jealous about all the attention I'm getting." She flopped back on the bed and then picked up the phone. "I'm going to tell Tasha about the necklace."

I *was* jealous.

About the jelly beans from Dad, but not the necklace. I couldn't, however, think of anything else to say.

*****

From Jade's private hospital room that night, we watched the fire on the five o'clock news. The news crew

at the TV studio called my efforts heroic. They put one of those big pictures up behind their desks. The photo was really of Jade, but I didn't care. It had my name, spelled correctly, underneath.

Then they showed portions of the footage. The KKSC cameraman had come back when he heard Sandra scream. He hadn't missed much of the action.

His sound picked up me yelling, "Drop and roll."

He filmed me throwing the towel on top of Jade and us rolling on the floor. At that point the newscaster had recovered enough to give commentary on the "hot" story. Good thing he did, because his shoulder blocked a portion of the camera so my kick to the firefighter's shin wasn't caught on film.

Next the TV showed Jade being loaded into an ambulance, much like the Ashley Dawn scene. Then the camera panned to Rand Knighton. "Just a minor accident," he said into the sno-cone. "No harm done to the set. The sprinklers were turned off in time to prevent water damage. Production will go on as scheduled. *Thoroughbred Fever* will not stop filming, even for a day . . ."

A minor accident? No harm done to the set? My sister is scarred for life, and it's a minor accident!

"Please turn it off," Jade said, falling back on a pile of pillows. "I want to forget all about it."

"OK." I gave in easily because Tasha was videotaping it for us.

Just as I picked up the TV remote control to turn it off, I saw Ryan come up from behind Rand, who was still promoting *Thoroughbred Fever.* Ryan lifted up two fingers behind the director's head. He was giving Mr. Knighton rabbit ears.

Ten

"I'm going to find Dad and your doctor," I explained to Jade as I left the hospital room. "I'm going to get them to stop talking so we can go." I picked up a small backpack from the chair next to the bed and gave it to her. "I brought you some clean clothes to go home in. They said tomorrow, right?"

She nodded; her eyes closed as she leaned back on the pillows.

Entering the hospital hallway, I was almost run down by two nurses pushing an old woman on a gurney. Stepping out of the way, I bumped into a short man, my elbow jabbing him in his ample stomach.

"Excuse me," I said.

"Certainly." He moved out of my way, sweeping one arm aside in a gesture to let me pass in front of him. In his outstretched hand was a small Bible.

I stared at the book. "Are you a priest?" I asked.

"No," the man in the dull brown suit said, "they wear black-and-white collars and usually make their rounds earlier in the day."

"Then what are you? Do you go around and talk to people who are dying?"

"Well," he said, "we're all dying, even if we're not in

the hospital. But I do counsel people who are sick or depressed. I'm a pastor."

I didn't really understand what he meant by everyone dying, so I figured he must know a lot.

"Have you read the whole Bible," I asked, "to the very last page?"

He nodded. "Several times."

"Can I pay you to talk to my sister, then? She's not depressed, and her burn will get better, but she's got one of those crystal things."

"Oh, New Age," he said, smiling. I got the idea he thought I was joking. "I'll talk to her, and I won't charge you a dime. Which room is hers?"

"Over here." I pointed. "She's not staying long, maybe just till the morning. You've got to talk to her—" I grabbed his arm and pushed him inside Jade's room. I felt as though I was losing my sister. If she wouldn't talk to me, maybe she'd listen to a pastor.

*****

I stalled Dad and Jade's doctor as long as I could by asking questions. Dad loves it when I'm interested in medical stuff. They told me they didn't know how bad Jade's burn was, that her skin might lose its normal color, but that she might not scar. Even if she did get to go home, she'd have to come back every day to have her bandage and medicine changed.

When Dad looked at his watch, I could stall no longer.

"I need to say good-bye to Jade," he said. We moved down the hall. Just as we got to the door, the short, round man in brown popped out of Jade's room as a rabbit hopping out its hole.

"She's asleep now," he said to me. Waving with his Bible, he hurried down the hall.

"Who was that?" Dad asked.

"A pastor." I opened Jade's door. Sure enough, the pastor's preaching had put Jade to sleep. She was even snoring.

*****

I tried to fall asleep on the drive home, but Dad kept asking questions about the fire that kept me awake—then and for many a night to come.

"Who would set fire to Jade?" he asked.

"No one could have known it was Jade," I said. "Nobody knew who Rand Knighton was going to send to makeup until about three minutes before Jade put on the smock."

"No one except Rand Knighton, then."

"Yeah." I hadn't thought of that before. "Why would he want Jade on fire?"

"What about this makeup artist, Sandra somebody . . ."

"I suppose she could have done it," I said, "but we met her just that day."

"Could she have been paid?"

"Who would pay her to hurt Jade? We're only fourteen."

"Where was Mrs. Kennett?" He turned the car onto our street. "She's supposed to watch you."

"She was busy." I didn't mention the fact that she had to find Ryan, who was roaming the halls.

"What if the fire starter thought it was going to be you wearing the smock? What then? Do you have any enemies?"

Sure I had enemies—people who were jealous that I

was in a movie, a girl I hurt last year by accidentally slamming my locker door on her finger. Tasha and I hadn't been on wonderful terms this year, but there was no one I thought would try to set me on fire. That was extreme.

When the car stopped in the garage, I was slow getting out.

A tall figure suddenly moved into the garage. It blocked the light coming from a fluorescent bulb, casting a long shadow over the car.

"Dad, duck!" I yelled and dove to the floor. If someone would burn Jade on purpose, then that same someone could come into our garage and club us on the head—or worse.

But Dad didn't exactly jump. He slowly turned and said, "What now, McKenna?"

"Hey," the figure called. "It's me, Ryan."

"Oh, hello there," Dad said, as if it was perfectly normal for teenage guys to pop up out of nowhere. I climbed out, a little angry at being so frightened, but so relieved that it was Ryan, I forgot I was ignoring him.

As Dad unlocked the door to the house, Ryan whispered to me, "I was going to call you, but I thought your phone might be bugged."

"Our phone bug—"

"Shhh. Don't let your dad hear, or he'll have a heart attack."

"Hear what?"

"Can we go in? It's cold."

"OK."

I took Ryan into the kitchen and gave him a glass of soda. Dad wandered into his study to sort through a stack of mail.

"I saw her at the studio," he said between gulps of

soda. "And I watched her drive away right before the fire broke out."

"Who is 'her'? Who did you see?"

"That blond girl. The one who quit."

"Ashley? You saw Ashley Dawn Saunders on the set? But she's suing Galaxy Studios for endangerment and psychological trauma. SAG is behind her."

"I know," he said. "That's why I followed her. She wasn't supposed to be there, now was she?"

We heard a thud come from Dad's study. It sounded as if he were pounding his fist on the desk. "I can't believe it!" he yelled.

I sprinted to the room with Ryan following. "What is it?"

"Read this!" He slid a large packet of papers across his desk and then pounded his fist once more.

With Ryan looking over my shoulder, I scanned the top letter. "Oh, no. Not you, too."

"That's right," Dad said. "Ashley's mother is suing me for a botched plastic surgery job. She claims I damaged Ashley's nasal passages. They want money for psychological damages because she couldn't breathe during the fire, and for another surgery to fix her sinuses."

"But she's fine!" Ryan said. "I saw her running—and running fast—to her car."

"Of course she's fine," Dad said. He laid his glasses on the table and rubbed between his eyebrows with his fingers. "The whole point of suing doctors is to get money. Physicians usually settle out of court, because if we let the case go before a jury, the jurors almost always care more about the patient. Juries see all doctors as money-hungry, and so they believe we're to blame."

"But you're not like that, Dad," I said.

"Well, I do make slightly more than minimum wage, and I am a plastic surgeon. Most people think all I do is fix up the rich and famous—that is, until their toddler falls through a window. Then I'm a hero because I patch up his face and hide the scars. . . . In Ashley's case, however, I revised her nose twice because she changed her mind. First it was one face, then another. That won't look good in court. Ashley's lawyer will say it took me so many times because I'm a bad surgeon."

"What are you going to do?" Ryan asked.

"Call *my* lawyers in the morning. I pay them to handle stuff like this," he said. "Actually, it's all in a day's work. I'm just upset because of Jade. Those fires make no sense."

"What if we prove that Ashley set the fire at the stage?" I asked. "Maybe she had this lawsuit planned from the beginning. Would that help you win the case?"

Dad sat forward and the tension creases on his forehead smoothed, as if my idea was a good one. But then he slumped back in his chair.

"No," he said. "Leave Ashley Saunders and her whole family alone. It could look as if we're trying to intimidate her. They could use that in court or press legal charges of harassment."

The clock on the bookshelf chimed ten. Dad hinted that it was time for Ryan to leave. "Ryan, should you call your mom or do you need me to take you home?"

"Yes, I'd like a ride. Thanks."

Ryan gave me a look that said, "We'll talk later." And they were out the door.

I locked the door. I checked every single window and quadruple-checked that the security system was set. Then I went to the phone. The machine registered thirty-five calls.

Might as well get this over with.

I sat down and listened to them all. Most were from fans calling to wish Jade a speedy recovery. I liked those. Two mean ones said we deserved to be in the fire. I didn't care for those. Three were from Tasha. All of them came after the five o'clock news.

I crawled into bed and prayed that Dad would come home safely. I was also worried that Ashley would come, torch in hand, and burn down the house. I spun my bracelet to remind myself that God was watching over me. Then I got to thinking . . . *If Ashley did set the fires, what good would it do her? Why would she want her movie career to end? Where did thirty-some-odd people get our home phone number? Why does that crystal necklace give me the creeps?*

Most of the questions I couldn't answer right then. But the last one I could. For the first time in weeks, I grabbed my Bible and began to read. Somewhere in that thick book lay the answer about the crystal.

Eleven

LaShondra found me the next morning as soon as she saw my blond head come through the studio door.

"Come along, now," she said, her hair bouncing as she moved. "We've got to move you right through makeup and wardrobe. You haven't been fitted yet, have you?"

I shook my head.

"Well, it's a good thing you're shorter than Ashley. If you were taller, we'd have to start from scratch. As it is, we'll make do."

The studio salon had been completely redecorated in less than twenty-four hours. New flooring and fresh paint had turned the room white with royal blue and yellow trim. The strong smell of paint covered up any lingering smoke fumes.

To put me at ease, Sandra chatted and clucked over me. And today, neither LaShondra nor Mrs. Kennett left. They stayed close; I suppose they were worried about more weird accidents.

"What was Ashley like?" I asked Sandra as she fastened a brand-new, right-out-of-the-package smock around my neck.

"Oh, honey," said Sandra, "that sounds morbid. You mean, what *is* she like?"

"No. I mean, what was she like on the set?"

She wet my face with a washcloth. "In here she was really picky. I had to do her hair just so, and then redo it three times. I bought a whole new line of lemon-smelling hair care products so she would be happy."

I checked on Mrs. Kennett and LaShondra by looking in the mirror. Ryan's mom was reading a book. LaShondra was going over the call sheet. "Do you always wear a smock?" I asked Sandra.

"Always. I've messed up too many outfits with this goop." She pointed to the array of jars and bottles on the dressing table.

Sandra tilted the chair so I could lean back. I closed my eyes and wondered, *Was Sandra the real target for the fire? Or is there something else I don't know about?*

I quietly submitted to having a light powder spread over my skin. But it didn't change the way I looked at all.

"I'm all done, except for the eyes," she said, handing me a box. "You need to put these on first."

"What's in this?"

"Contacts."

"But I see fine."

"Didn't they tell you? Not only are you a blond for this movie, but your eyes are blue."

*****

After my hair was finished and the blow-dryer was off with no way to spark another fire, Mrs. Kennett went to use the phone because her pager had gone off. LaShondra took me to my dressing room. I half expected Ashley's name to be on the door, but instead "Cassidy" was written on a note card held in a little brass bracket. The actors could change, but the role stayed the same.

The tiny room was stuffed with a table, a small bed,

and a plastic wastepaper basket. "Here are your clothes!" LaShondra said, sweeping her arm in the direction of a tiny closet. Neatly hung on plastic coat hangers was an English riding outfit. On a shelf sat an acorn-shaped helmet and black boots. "Try these on. I'll send up someone from wardrobe to check the fit." She bebopped out, closing the door behind her.

Seeing the costume helped me remember I wasn't here just to find out if Ashley had set the fires. I had two scenes to shoot. After pulling on the clothes and cramming my feet into the boots, I opened the door and looked down the hall. No sign of LaShondra.

There was nothing else to do but stare in the mirror. I barely recognized myself in the tailored riding clothes. A white silk shirt and fitted black pants turned me into a Miss Prissy.

And I still hadn't gotten used to the blond hair. Having something light instead of dark framing my face made my mouth and eyes appear brighter. As for the contacts, I couldn't even feel them. They were ultrathin. "Can't have crying actors, now, can we?" Sandra had said. But the blue color totally changed my face. It softened.

"Typical actor," said a voice from the doorway. "Can't take your eyes off yourself. That blond hair and white shirt make you look like an angel."

I turned to find Snap Herez. Since I'm not allowed to watch soaps, I'd never seen him act. But I recognized his face from a poster inside Tasha's locker. He was wearing a simple costume—jeans, white tank T-shirt, work boots, and an unshaved face.

"We're on in twenty minutes. Can I take you to the stable set?" he asked.

Even though he was leaning against my doorway smiling, the tilt of his eyebrows and the square of his jaw

made him look mischievous. If I indeed looked like an angel, he looked every bit a demon.

I knew from reading my call sheet that I was in a scene with him that morning. In fact, most of my scenes included him. He played a stable boy named Sammy who was helping Cassidy's Aunt Savannah drug horses so they would run faster in races.

"Excuse me," Snap said, stepping into the dressing room. He snapped his fingers in front of my face. "Can I take you to the stable set?"

I realized I hadn't answered his question. "Oh, I'm sorry. I was lost in thought. I'm McKenna James."

"I know," he said. "I've seen film clips, and I watched the KKSC news last night. You're well on your way to being a legend. Lucky for you the cameraman filmed your brave rescue."

"If I were lucky," I said, "my sister wouldn't be in the hospital."

"I didn't mean to imply that you did it on purpose," he laughed. "But come on, you have to admit the timing was perfect. In comes this camera crew and *POOF!* your sister goes up in smoke. For an actor, being in the news is good news."

"I've got to get fitted. You'd better get back to the set . . ." I pretended I didn't know his name.

"Snap. Snap Herez. Otherwise known as 'Sam.' " He bowed. "Your humble stable servant, Miss Cassidy Kennedy." As he turned, I saw a tattoo on the back of his shoulder. It was a circle with white and black swirls. Two dots of the opposite color in each swirl made them look like fish trapped in a bowl. I had no idea what it meant.

I could see why Tasha and Jade liked him. It was nice of him to come talk to me, to make me feel part of the movie. But I also wanted to know where he had been when the fires started.

Twelve

LaShondra came back with a wardrobe assistant named Rita.

The plump, happy woman pinched and pulled at the clothes.

"We're fine with these," she said. "Just keep the trousers tucked inside the boots; that hides the extra length nicely." Next, her light-brown hands and a yellow tape measure recorded my dimensions: neck, bust, waist, arms, and legs. As Rita wrapped the tape around me like a boa constrictor, I asked more questions.

"Wasn't the first fire started in Ashley's dressing room?" I asked. "This room looks fine to me."

"Oh, it wasn't this room," LaShondra said, writing my measurements down on a clipboard as the other woman called out the numbers. "That room has been closed."

"Which one is it?" I asked.

"Don't go in there," LaShondra warned. "But if you look down the hall to the right, it's the one with the broken door. You can see inside from the doorway, which is roped off. It's nasty. The arson investigator asked us not to remodel it, because of yesterday's fire. He wasn't too happy we already fixed up the makeup salon. He'll go over it for more clues. By the way . . ."

"Yes?"

"Sometime today he's going to want to question you about the smock and the fire and all. Also, he heard about some guy who was on the set, your boyfriend . . ."

"Oh, he's not my boyfriend," I said. "He's Mrs. Kennett's son."

"I understand now," LaShondra said. "Completely." She gave Rita a knowing look with raised eyebrows and a wink. I could tell she thought I was trying to hide something. Adults try to find puppy love anywhere.

Rita measured from my knee to the floor. "Is Jade the same size as you are?"

"Yes," I said. "Exactly."

Rita was almost done. I wanted a look at that dressing room before LaShondra took me to the set.

"Uh, is it all right if I use the restroom now?"

*****

I sneaked down the hall to the site of the fire. Trashed was an understatement. Totaled, destroyed, fried—those were better words to describe the room.

I could see inside from behind the rope, but I stepped over it to get a better look. Ashley's dressing room was twice the size of mine and Jade's. All that was left of the bed, desk, and chair was blackened, skeletal pieces of wood. Careful not to stir up a lot of soot, I searched everything, even checking under what had been the mattress.

"What are you looking for? A matchbook with a phone number written inside?"

I zipped around. I hadn't heard anyone sneak up on me. The question had been asked by a man in a taupe suit and a flowered tie. His gray hair was cut slanted

across his forehead. The slope matched his smile, tilted up to the left.

"I, I don't really know . . . ," I said. "Maybe a clue?"

"You must be McKenzie—"

"McKenna James," I corrected him. "And you are?"

"Barney. Barney Neverland. Arson investigator." His voice was raspy like a smoker's. I wondered if it had gotten that way breathing fumes from fires.

"Do you know how this fire was set?"

"Well, McKenna," he said. "I'll let you see if you can figure it out. Every fire leaves a story. What do you think the beginning of this story was?"

"The desk?" I thought it would catch on fire quickly.

"Uh-uh." He shook his head. "What's missing?"

"The blanket!" I could see it now. The bed had caught on fire from the blanket, probably at the foot of the bed. The bottom of the mattress could still be recognized. It spread to the desk from the carpet, which was burnt near both pieces of furniture.

"Ashley said she was asleep when the fire detector went off," the investigator said. "The flames never got to her feet. That's the most important clue I've found."

"Why?"

"It was a brand-spanking-new fire detector. And there isn't one in any of the other rooms."

I'll bet Ashley is lying. Maybe she set the fire and waited till it looked dangerous and then ran out of the room. We're gonna prove she did it yet.

"If you can figure out a reason someone would set a fire with pyro fluid and then make sure the blaze was detected, you let me know, Miss James." I stared at the room, thinking about Ashley and her lawsuits. When I turned around to ask what pyro fluid was, Barney Neverland had gone as quietly as he had come.

Thirteen

I'm fourteen, so I've been around a while. But it was obvious I could turn eighteen, twenty even, before Mr. Knighton would stop treating me like a little kid. Some people are just like that.

We were almost alone on the horse stall set, working through my scene. By "almost alone" I mean only one soundman and the DP were there too. If fewer than five people are around on set, you're practically in solitary confinement.

"Do you know your lines, honey?" Mr. Knighton asked.

Thanks to Jade's tape, I knew them better than the writer did. But I didn't tell him that, since he *was* the scriptwriter. He wouldn't listen. I just smiled and nodded.

"This first scene is short, and we've already got most of it from before. The crew knows where everything should be. We just need to reshoot the parts Ashley already did. You and Sam are meeting for the first time. You come in when he's not expecting you. He tries to hide the syringe—do you know what that is?"

'I think so," I said flatly, not telling him my dad's occupation or that I had used one as a weapon last summer.

"OK," he continued, "you walk in and ask Sam what's behind his back, but you really don't know yet that he's injecting the horses, giving them shots. Got it, sweetie?"

"Got it."

"LaShondra!" Rand Knighton called over his shoulder. The girl bounced in, her beaded braids and flowered vest flapping. She must have been waiting just around the corner.

"Get Sammy and the horse in here, OK?"

"Right away."

The horse came first. He was led by the horse wrangler who was wearing a T-shirt, boots, and jeans. This one wasn't over six feet tall, he didn't smile, and he loved that horse. He spoke to the animal in Spanish coos and led him slowly into the set.

Snap followed.

Before I knew it, the entire movie crew had surrounded us.

Outside the set window, light technicians—called grips—were fixing special colored cellophane screens and lights to make it look like sunrise. Three men standing on ladders looked down on us; one was holding a long pole called a "boom" for the microphone; the others were fiddling with something. One more technician worried about the soundboard. A woman was wandering around with a pitchfork and a water bucket. Sandra came to check our makeup.

"You'll do fine," she whispered to me, powdering my face. She reapplied my lip gloss and went to work on Snap. She took out a photo album and compared his look with the snapshots. She put more goop on his hair to slick it back. She spent five minutes just parting it and trimming his neck hairs.

Mr. Knighton sat in a director's chair with "Galaxy

Studios" written on the back. He spoke to the AD, who got out his bullhorn and called for a root beer. In a flash an older teen in khakis and a polo shirt brought a can of soda. The AD pointed at Knighton. The courier extended it to the director.

"What's this?" Knighton said. "I asked for a root beer. This is ginger ale."

"Craft services was out of root beer . . ."

"And you're out of a job." He waved his arm to dismiss the gofer. "Tell the caterer to get root beer before lunch."

Without a word, the young man left.

I didn't have time to think about the injustice of it all, because Knighton waved to a man wearing headphones.

"Action!" called the AD.

That's when I realized there would be no rehearsal. The director might talk to me as if I were a baby, but he certainly expected me to act like an adult. When I had said, "Got it," that was the end of my training. Period.

Thank goodness Snap has the first line.

We shot the scene six times, all for footage of me to replace Ashley's.

I had been worried the horse would kick me, but he was calm as ever. In between takes, the horse wrangler would come in and rub its ears.

After each scene, Mr. Knighton and the DP watched the film again through a little monitor set up near the soundboard. When that scene was wrapped up, Mr. Knighton talked to the AD, who barked some orders in the microphone. The crew vanished, rolling their cameras away and packing boxes to move to the next set.

Mr. Knighton squatted to be on eye-level with me. "That was a very good job, honey." He patted my head, a gesture annoying to anyone over three years old. "Run

along now and find LaShondra so you won't get lost."

"Do you have kids?" I asked him, wondering how he could be so clueless about how to treat a teen.

"No," he said.

Figures.

*****

I searched the studio and couldn't find LaShondra, so I went back to the set. The horse, the wrangler, and the strong smell of the animal were the only things left.

"Hi!" I said to the horse's caretaker. "May I pet him?"

"Sure," he said. His accent made the *s* sound like *ch.* "He's a good boy, aren't you, *amigo?*" He slapped the horse's rump.

I rubbed the beast's nose, wishing Jade were there. "I know his name is Thunderbolt for the movie," I said. "But what is it really?"

"Charlie."

"Can he run fast?"

"Oh, no, girl," he said. "He would be poor if he were a race horse. No, no, no. He's a good boy, won't bite, won't kick. Perfect for a movie horse. Pretty, too. . . ."

"You take good care of him," I said, running my hand across his glossy coat. "Anyone can see that you care about animals."

The comment took him by surprise. He looked down and didn't say anything. I didn't know his name, and I was feeling weird, as if I should have kept my lips closed. I turned to leave.

"No," the man said, "don't go. You may get into trouble here. If you need help, you just see me. I owe you a favor."

"Why? You don't even know me."

At first I didn't think he was going to answer. He put Charlie's halter on over the silky ears and hooked a lead rope to it. But as he led the horse out of the stall, he said, "In this business, you've got to know who your friends are. I'm letting you know that you can count on me."

That didn't answer my question. If I had an instant friend, I wanted to how I'd done it. "But why *me?*"

"You're the first person in six weeks who has said something nice to me." He said it matter-of-factly, no self-pity. "No one else even knows I speak English. They've never bothered to ask."

Fourteen

I went back to my dressing room in search of LaShondra or Mrs. Kennett. Neither was there. No notes to tell me what to do. *Well, until they find me, I'll find out more about Ashley.*

My first interview would be with Snap. He had worked closely with her on *Seems Like Eternity*, had been here the day of the fire, and might have seen her leaving the studio the day before. I checked my call sheet. Neither one of us had to report to the set for a half hour.

I knocked on his dressing room door.

"Come on in, McKenna," he called.

Opening the door, I heard soft piano music and smelled something smoky sweet. "How did you know who it was?"

"You're the only other actor working this morning," he said. He was sitting on the bed. From the way his hair was rumpled, I could tell he had been lying down.

"Plus," he continued, "I figured you would want to talk over our next scene. As you noticed earlier, Rand isn't one for long rehearsals. He just sort of throws actors into the fire to heat things up."

Leaving the door wide open, I stepped farther inside

and looked around. Snap had been there more than a day. His room looked lived in. A boom box, TV, and cellular phone sat on his dressing table. The sweet, smoky smell came from something burning in an ashtray near the bed.

I didn't know how best to ask about Ashley, so I just said, "Is our next scene difficult?"

"Nope."

"Did I do OK earlier?"

"You'll know when you do something wrong," he laughed.

I didn't like the sound of that. I remembered Claude and Beatrice's warning that Mr. Knighton thinks he's a god. But I saw my chance to turn the conversation toward Ashley.

"Did Ashley do a good job?"

"Let's just say she should stick to soaps."

"Then why did Ms. Haveshire hire her?" I asked.

"Ashley has been hounding her, and every other casting director around, for at least a year. All of a sudden, Ashley lands this great role—which she blew."

The smell of the incense burning began to give me a headache. I sniffed and wrinkled my nose.

"Not used to this, I can see," he said, picking up the little musty triangle and turning it over in the ashtray. The smoldering stopped.

"What is that for?"

"Oh, the music and this stuff help me meditate. To keep me centered. I act better when I'm in tune."

We had talked about centering in my acting classes as a way to focus on our characters' feelings. But I had this weird feeling that he meant it differently. This stuff was like the crystal.

"Galaxy Studios sent my sister a crystal—"

"Yeah, a lot of us are into this stuff. It's all part of the New Age that's here. I'm glad to see you've got an open mind . . ."

"What was the crystal for?"

"Crystals have healing powers. They help spiritual energy converge, and the body to become, well, less physical. It allows for immaterial unification with the universe."

Is he serious?! His talk was really making my head pound. But I had to ask about the tattoo. "What does that mark on your shoulder mean?"

"That," he said, inspecting it by turning his shoulder and craning his neck around, "is an Eastern symbol of good and evil. Two equal forces that make the whole of life."

"You don't believe that good is stronger?" I asked. Even before I believed in God, I had always sensed there was Something good out there.

"No," he said. "One can't exist without the other. In many ways good is evil, and evil is good. It just depends on your interpretation."

"So, you're saying there is no right or wrong?" I asked, not really believing I was hearing right.

"I guess so. That's an old-fashioned idea. All it produces is guilt. Each person must seek his own path without judgement from others. You have to do what you think is right."

"Well, I've got to go find LaShondra. . . ." I said, making a hasty exit.

God sure made it clear what was right and wrong in the Old Testament. I know at least that much.

*****

LaShondra came bounding into my dressing room. "Let me show you where the set classroom is on the way to the set," she offered. "You were supposed to be there between your scenes. You have to get in at least three hours of tutoring a day." No apologies. No explanations. No excuses.

I followed her down the hall. It wasn't a schoolroom. Just some tables and metal folding chairs. The only thing unusual about it was the old lady. She was asleep, head tilted forward onto her well-rounded chest.

"That's old Mrs. Bixby," LaShondra said. "She used to be a dancer, and a good one. Now she's a set teacher. She'll help you with your homework. . . . You did bring some, didn't you?"

"I can work on English today," I said. "I have an essay due." I tried to picture Mrs. Bixby dancing anywhere. *With an elephant maybe.*

Without waking her, LaShondra and I headed toward the set.

"LaShondra, where is Mrs. Kennett?" I hadn't seen her after she went to call Jade early in the morning.

"We'll talk about that later," she said. "Stay happy and don't think about her; just concentrate on your next scene."

"But where is she?" I said. "She's supposed to be here the whole time."

"Chill out. There's plenty of time to worry about that after the scene," LaShondra said. "We really don't want to be late." She slowed her voice and said each of the next words with chopped pronunciation. "We do not want to upset Mr. Knighton?" The way she stated the fact like a question made me nervous. I couldn't get that root beer versus ginger ale incident out of my mind. Would I be fired for any simple mistake too?

Fifteen

This time, the set was ready before I got there. Mr. Knighton was dismissing the stand-ins as LaShondra and I walked in. The script supervisor called to LaShondra, and I was left alone. Immediately, the set firefighter stood beside me and tapped my shoulder.

"McKenna?" he asked.

I nodded.

"I hope," he said in a kind, gentle voice, "that I didn't hurt you when I moved you out of the way yesterday. I wanted to apologize earlier, but you were busy."

I must have been, because I hadn't noticed him earlier in the day. I looked up at him then. He was wearing a blue uniform with a Galaxy Studio patch on the front. The newscaster had called him Marcus Harris.

"I hope I didn't hurt you when I kicked you in the shin." I smiled. I was kind of embarrassed about the whole thing. And I was actually glad a firefighter was on the set. He certainly earned his salary.

"Nope," he said. "That kick is our little secret. The only person I told was dear ol' ma, and there's no telltale bruise." He held out his hand. "Friends?" he asked.

"Friends."

"Can I join this little club?" Barney Neverland's ques-

tion was the first I'd noticed him. He had sneaked up on us.

"I've got some questions for you, Harris," the arson investigator added. "Why would someone plan a fire when they knew a news crew was going to be at the studio?"

"Sounds like a textbook case," Marcus said. "Fire setters are often just asking for attention. It's their cry for help."

"That's right," the older man's raspy voice answered.

"McKenna, you got a lot of media attention from yesterday's fire. Have you seen today's paper?"

He pulled a copy of the *Los Angeles Times* from under his arm and dropped it on a chair. My face looked up from the Metro section.

The headline read, "McKenna and Jade James' career off to a hot start on *Thoroughbred Fever* set."

Does he think I set the fire?

I was going to ask Mr. Neverland the question, but when I looked up, he was gone, melted into the crowd of workers.

*****

"McKenna!"

I turned my head in the direction of the set. The golden-haired director who had just called my name was striding toward me. Either he had some physical pain like a hot coal in his shoe or he was angry. Nothing else would make his tan face scrunch up like a shriveled apple.

Oh, Lord, I prayed, *I've been warned this was coming. Please help me be calm.*

I decided to ignore his look and pretend everything

was just fine. "Hi, are we ready to go?" I said in my most cheerleader-type voice. "This is going to be a great scene."

"If it is, it will be with no help from you," he spat.

I made a mental note not to get mad if he ever treated me like a little kid again. His anger was worse multiplied by a million.

"Did I do something wrong?" I asked as if I were an angel. I hoped he would soften when he saw my new blue eyes.

Acting innocent didn't work.

"You're in the wrong clothes," he snapped.

LaShondra, the dear woman, rushed over to help, or so I thought.

"Mr. Knighton," she said, "I was going to mention this sooner, but I didn't want to upset you. See, McKenna ran away for about an hour. We couldn't find her anywhere."

Did I hear that right? I disappeared? Where was she?

"I told you to go find her," Knighton said to me. "I'm the director; you do as you're told."

I was in a fix. I had searched for LaShondra, but not very hard. So it was partially my fault I was in the wrong clothes. But LaShondra hadn't mentioned a wardrobe change, and there had been no new clothes in my dressing room.

Mr. Knighton had a long finger, which he waved in front of my face. "Do you know how much money you waste every minute you hold up filming?" His finger then jabbed at his watch. "What kind of a stupid stunt is this?" he asked, grabbing the silk sleeve of the riding outfit.

I've heard you aren't supposed to stare down a bear. And I figured the same could be said for grizzlyish

directors. I turned my head away from his eyes and met LaShondra's.

As she met my gaze, she tilted her head, and the braids and beads covered her face, too. *She can't look me in the eye. She feels guilty.* Knighton wasn't going to get the truth from her. And if I tried to blame her, I'd look like a whiny tattletale. LaShondra pulled out a cell phone, her long black tassels cascading over her hand.

I could sense the crew's attention. Everyone watched more carefully now than when I was acting. It was as if someone had hit the pause button on the VCR and the audience was waiting for the show to continue. Had this happened at school, the kids would have circled around and started chanting, "Fight. Fight. Fight."

I was trapped. I couldn't think of a thing to say that wouldn't put my word against LaShondra's or be a complete lie. And instead of quieting him, my silence made Rand Knighton grow taller and angrier. He filled his chest to huff and puff and blow me down. His left arm raised.

Afraid of his temper, I took a step back because I expected him to slap me. *Where are you when I need you, Mrs. Kennett?*

A voice coughed out, "Thank you, Mr. Knighton!" Everyone turned to see Barney Neverland. "I see you've got the crew assembled, just as I asked you to. I've got several questions about yesterday's fire." His rough words sounded sweeter than a Hershey's Kiss. "I've already interviewed McKenna," he said, "so she can go ahead and change."

I didn't wait for Mr. Knighton's answer. I heard my cue and I took it, running all the way to wardrobe.

*****

Rita was ready for me. "LaShondra just called." She shoved a pile of clothes into my arms. "Hurry. This isn't finished, but it'll have to do. Watch for pins in the waistband of the pants."

I dropped the clothes on a chair. "Let me borrow the phone first," I said. I didn't wait for her to say yes. I just grabbed it off of her belt and dialed the Kennetts'.

There was no answer. I left a message and then called dad's voice mail, using my special emergency code.

"Someone has got to come get me," I recorded. "Mrs. Kennett is gone, kidnapped maybe, and Mr. Knighton has gone crazy."

Then I kicked off my boots and almost tore off the clothes. I pulled on the new jockey's outfit. It was purple and yellow silk. Bright, gaudy, and shiny. Rita shoved a yellow cap into my hands.

"It should be large enough," she said. "Ashley's head is bigger than yours."

A new pair of boots, lighter and more comfortable, carried me back to the set faster than I had left it. I pushed past a few set carpenters in the halls leading down to the newly constructed set.

I joined the crowd listening to Barney. He saw me, winked, and said to the crew, "If you think of any other details you may have forgotten to mention about that morning, especially about strangers on the set, please let me know."

Sixteen

Rand Knighton could change his moods quicker than I could flip channels with a remote. After Mr. Neverland finished talking to the crew about yesterday's fire, the director was fine, relaxed, munching away on some candy and yogurt-covered pretzels. I didn't, however, ask him to share.

While the crew was waiting for the AD and the special-effects technician to finish talking, Snap Herez told me I wouldn't get to see an explosion, because that had been filmed while Ashley was around. But we would be filming in the middle of smoke. The scene was supposed to look like the stall next to us was on fire.

"What does USMC stand for?" I asked Snap.

"United States Marine Corps. Why?"

I pointed to the tattoo on the special-effects man's right biceps.

"Yeah, that's Al. He's ex-military, all right. Knows how to blow up bridges and buildings, cars and houses. He's the best TD—technical director—for explosions and pyrotechnics around, Knighton says. Al did all the fires and bombings in that last Vietnam movie."

Al had been out of the military a long time by the look and length of his reddish-brown-and-gray hair. It

hung halfway down his back in a scraggly ponytail. I guessed the black boxes with brass locks that Al's teenaged assistants guarded stored explosives and other weird stuff. The guy and girl each wore black T-shirts marked "Galaxy Studios Special Effects Crew," and they had the trunks and boxes roped off, with signs that said, "No Smoking."

"Hey," Snap said, "Knighton wants us."

The director was motioning to us with a pretzel pinched between thumb and index finger. LaShondra, clipboard on hip, came over to check my costume as Snap and I headed for the center of the set. "It's the right one, McKenna."

No thanks to you, I thought. But I smiled at her anyway, hoping to let the whole thing blow over.

"Do you know where LaShondra was earlier?" Snap asked, as she walked away.

I shook my head.

"I can make a good guess."

My eyebrow raised to ask him where.

"She's usually tucked away in a trailer somewhere," he said. "Sometimes she gets migraine headaches and the heat and the lights of the set are just too much for her."

"Does Mr. Knighton know?" I asked.

"I doubt it," Snap said, "or LaShondra would have said something this morning when you were taking the heat."

I was still angry, but sort of felt sorry for her.

"Why doesn't she go to the doctor?"

"Been there, done that," Snap said. "What she really needs is to get to a higher plane."

"So you're admitting that the pain is a bad thing." I had him trapped. For such a handsome head, there wasn't

much inside if he thought that there was really no right or wrong.

"Well," he said, catching on that I was trying to get him to admit some things were just plain old evil, "pain can be good if it points you toward enlightenment."

"But then *un*enlightenment is bad," I said. "I just won't believe that nothing is bad. There's got to be something you'd call evil."

He didn't answer because the director and crew were ready for us. The short rehearsal went smoothly. Snap's makeup and hair matched the Polaroids. Sandra fiddled with my hair a tad.

When it was time for the smoke to begin wafting in, Snap pulled me aside. "McKenna, work with me on this scene," he said. "It'll be hard for the film editors to get this scene right if we have a lot of takes. The smoke billows in and out, and they need to match its thickness. Plus, we'll already have to redo the lines because of the noise of the fans. Knighton threw a fit the day Ashley did it—"

"And you don't want that to happen again. Got it." I wished he hadn't said anything. I looked at my hand; it was shaking.

The ex-Marine and an assistant turned on fans hooked up to cans of mineral oil. The oil would be heated up to create "smoke" that didn't sting the eyes. The smoke would be pumped by hand into the fans, which would blow the mist across the set.

Marcus Harris inspected the third fan. Even before the smoke wafted onto the set, my shaking hands began to sweat when I remembered yesterday's fire. Would Marcus remember too? Would the person who set it? I sent a silent prayer to God, thanking Him that with today's smoke there would be no fire.

I looked around for Mr. Neverland. I almost didn't see him because he was in the middle of a cluster of crew members. He was listening, no doubt, should someone want to talk without the director hearing. Watching, too, to see if Marcus did anything suspicious. All in all, it was a short scene. To put me in instead of Ashley, they had rebuilt the whole set. I was to come in on Sam, who was setting the fire in the stall, trying to destroy the stables to ruin Aunt Savannah's fortune.

We exchanged our lines with no major problems. Knighton stopped us here and there for minor adjustments, telling me once not to let my voice shake. I didn't let it get to me. And during the filming, Snap's calm helped me stay focused on acting. Knighton yelled at one grip and the assistant DP when a camera dolly knocked over a spotlight, cracking the bulb.

But once the light was replaced, we were back to filming. My character pointed out the imaginary stall window. "Look, Thunderbolt has escaped!"

Snap ended the scene with, "But *you* won't!" And he pulled out a gun from underneath his T-shirt, pointing it at my chest.

The final "Cut!" was called. Knighton watched the scene on a special monitor that records what the camera sees. He nodded, and it was over.

Afterward, I decided to clear out. I didn't want to talk to Knighton, and I was worried about what to say to LaShondra. I stuck my hand in my pocket, looking for my ID bracelet so I could put it back on. But it was in the other pants, the ones I had taken off in such a rush. Instead, I found a handful of paper scraps. They were fuzzy around the edges and clumped together. I figured the pants had been dry-cleaned since Ashley had worn them last, and the chemicals had softened the paper.

I gently picked at the papers until the pieces separated. Then I started to put the puzzle together. "Wait for me in your dressing room," it read. The note was signed, "You know who."

I did not know who. And I didn't know if the note was meant for me or had been left for Ashley the last time she wore the costume. I wadded up the paper to throw it away, and then thought I'd keep it, just in case You Know Who showed up.

Seventeen

As it turned out, I didn't make it to the dressing room. Dad found me first. The vein on his forehead was bulging when he grabbed my arm as I walked out of the studio doors. Whenever Dad gets angry, a blue blood vessel shaped like a *Y* pops out between his eyebrows. So I can tell when he's mad and trying to hide it. He was trying to hide it now.

"You're mad," I said.

"No, I'm not. I'm just a bit frustrated that I had to leave work," he said. "You'd know if I were really angry." He hadn't put his car keys back in his pocket; they jingled as they dangled from his finger. Maybe I could get him to leave quickly.

"I'm all done filming today." I grabbed his arm to turn him away from the set and toward the dressing room.

"Good. Where is Rand Knighton?" He shoved the keys in his pocket.

"Oh, you don't want to waste time talking to him," I said. "Let's go to the hospital and visit Jade."

"Wait a minute, McKenna," he said. "I'm only here because *you* left a message that said Mrs. Kennett had been kidnapped and that Rand Knighton was crazy."

I had said that, hadn't I?

I had forgotten all about the message once the filming started. But I didn't want him talking to the director. Practically nobody talked to him while he was working.

"Well," I said to Dad, "everything with Mr. Knighton is all worked out now."

"Then where is Mrs. Kennett?" he answered. "A woman I've hired to watch you vanishes the day after your twin sister almost burns to death. You want me to overlook that minor detail? . . . I don't think so."

"You could ask LaShondra, the talent coordinator. She's supposed to know everything."

"I already called her. She said Mrs. Kennett got permission from the director to leave."

All out of ideas on how to change his mind, I walked back with him to the set.

"This is the stable where we were just filming," I told my dad. "There was smoke all over the place. I'll check over there. . . ." Despite wanting to see the director, my dad slowed down to inspect the set with its lights, flags, and electrical cords.

I came up behind Mr. Knighton and Al at the prop station, a spot where all the set decorations and other objects needed for a scene were stored.

"Well, I don't know how you got the wrong call sheet," Knighton was saying to the Marine. "We haven't got time to figure it out. We're not doing any more explosions. And I don't need a technical director for a little bit of smoke."

Knighton suddenly tuned in to my presence. He glanced at me and turned again to Al, saying, "Well, you'll be paid for your time. Sorry about the mix-up. I'm sure the missing gas canisters and plastic will show up. Someone probably knew what they were and stored

them in a safe place."

Al nodded and left, grabbing a black trunk on his way out. He passed my dad who had come to stand next to me.

Knighton, finished with that business, addressed us. "Well, hello, McKenna," he said to me. "And who is this?"

My dad offered a hand to the director. "I'm Darren James," Dad said, shaking Knighton's hand.

"What can I do for you?" Mr. Knighton, a tame grizzly now, bared his teeth in a smile.

"It seems we have a small problem with McKenna's personal manager, Lorraine Kennett, . . ." Dad began.

I saw Barney Neverland in the living room set. *Should I stay and listen to Dad, or go tell the investigator about the missing gas canisters?*

I could hear Dad later; I darted away to follow Neverland. "See you," I called over my shoulder. But Dad and the director didn't pay attention to me. Already they were talking in hushed tones.

*****

The fire investigator was wandering around the set, picking up props, opening drawers. "Hey, look at this, McKenna." Mr. Neverland tapped the fireplace. "This isn't brick. It's plastic."

"The grand piano is fake too," I said. "They don't want to have to move a real one. I saw them assembling it."

"Well I'll be." He stuck his head inside. "It's hollow," he chuckled. "No strings attached."

On the catwalk above us, a grip was adjusting a light. The clanking sound of the metal clamp against the pipe

holding the light made me nervous. I looked up, happy to see sprinklers among the lights and pulleys. I moved out from underneath him just in case.

"Maybe I should hire a bodyguard," I said. "That fire yesterday makes me think a blaze of fire will burn the place down any second."

"You're right to be worried, McKenna," Mr. Neverland said. He raised one fuzzy gray-and-white eyebrow above a concerned eye. "I'm worried myself. Two crimes of arson in two weeks. That doesn't look good. And four months ago on another set, there was a small electrical fire. It was a lot like the ones here."

"How?"

"Well," the arson investigator said, "someone started a blaze on a day that a lot of construction was going on. More than fifty carpenters had been on the set." He pulled out a little spiral pad to check his notes. "It was an easily contained fire with lots of smoke. But there was also a TV news crew. . . . That the news was there on the day Ashley's dressing room went up *and* when Jade caught fire—that's not just chance. Someone planned it that way."

"I still don't get it," I said. "If I were going to start a fire, which I wouldn't, I wouldn't want a crime on film. It's too easy to get caught. . . ."

I thought about Ashley. I thought about the guy who had dared to give Mr. Knighton a ginger ale, and the ignored horse wrangler. A lot of people—dozens maybe—could be angry or bitter at Knighton if he always treated people so harshly. Then I thought about Mr. Knighton himself, whether he'd get publicity for the movie by hurting people. There were other motives to set a fire besides wanting attention.

"McKenna?" Neverland crouched low so that no one

passing through the set by chance could hear him. "Could you find out if Marcus Harris is a nice guy and what his friends think about him?"

"Why? That's your job." I hadn't said yes, and I hadn't said no.

"Because no one will tell me the truth. I'm the investigator, and, well, you could probably find out from some friends in the business."

"Why are you so stuck on Marcus as the one?" I crossed my arms across my chest.

"Because," he said, sitting back on his heels, "Marcus was the firefighter on the set for the other fire I mentioned. He was given a medal, and a documentary company is going to make a movie about his rescues. . . . I'd say that fire was good business for him. Maybe he's pushing his own luck."

"You really think he set those fires himself?"

"Well, he's a hero, now, isn't he?" the investigator speculated. "He's the only one who has come out ahead."

Marcus had been nice and polite to me. I couldn't see him as an arsonist, someone who would hurt Jade or Ashley just to rescue one of them.

"But I got the credit for saving Jade," I said, defending a man I hardly knew.

"Exactly. But that was an accident. I'm afraid he might be jealous. You be careful, McKenna. And a bodyguard might not be a bad idea."

"If you're so sure Marcus did it, why don't you arrest him?"

"Because I don't have any proof . . . yet."

"Would it be proof enough if you caught him with gas cans stolen from the pyro guy?"

"Gas canisters? No, anyone can buy those at a hard-

ware store. It's the stuff plumbers use to heat pipes, or your dad might use some in his barbecue."

"OK. What about a trunk full of missing plastic?"

The word *plastic* got Neverland's attention.

"Did you say plastic?" he asked.

I nodded.

"The TD's plastic is missing?" He ran his fingers through his hair.

"Yeah," I said, "Snap said he blew up a horse stable last week. Lots of people watched him do it."

"Do you know what plastic is, McKenna?"

I shook my head.

"It's basically an explosion waiting to happen. And if Al uses the same stuff they do in the military, one trunkful is strong enough to blow up the whole studio."

Eighteen

You don't ask your dad questions about how much hair he's losing or why he spends forever locked in the bathroom reading newspapers, but I figured a question about Mrs. Kennett and Mr. Knighton would be OK.

I figured wrong.

We were driving to visit Jade in the hospital when he gave me the same message LaShondra had—don't talk about Mrs. Kennett.

"We'll talk about it when I've had a chance to talk to Mrs. Kennett," he said. It wasn't so much the words, but the way he said them that told me I was in for a wait. He'd probably rather talk about sex first.

He pulled the car over at a drugstore to buy Jade some stuff she wanted for her last day in the hospital.

As I wandered up and down the aisles, pushing a cart and choosing candy bars and cola, I noticed a young clerk following me. At least I thought he was watching. It didn't "just happen" that he had to stock the candy, slippers, makeup, and magazine sections the exact time I was in those aisles. I couldn't miss that mustard-yellow smock even if I wanted to, and I did. I hate it when store people assume I'm shoplifting just because I'm a teen.

To give him what he was looking for, I casually picked up a roll of peppermints and half-hid them in my hand. Then I sped my legs and the cart around a corner and waited for him to follow in turn. As he whipped around the aisle and almost rammed into me, I saw his name tag.

"What can I do for you, Ravi?" I asked, leaning against the canned vegetable display, casually tossing the breath mints up in the air.

"Uh . . . well . . . ," he said. Though he mumbled, his accent hinted he or his parents were from someplace like Pakistan or Saudi Arabia. His skin was a deep brown, and a flush warmed his face. Balls of sweat popped out like the bumps on a cucumber rind.

"Did you think I wasn't going to pay for this?" I waved the small roll of candies in front of his face. "I have my own credit card *and* my dad's here to pay for anything I want."

"It is not what you are thinking—I *was* following you," he said. "I'd like to get your autograph for my little sisters. They are twins too, and I bring them home the ads for Swan Softie products with your pictures on them."

"Why didn't you just ask me for it instead of sneaking around?"

"The hair. I couldn't tell if you were you or not," he said. "It hasn't been that color before, has it? And I thought your eyes were green." He leaned forward as if to make sure I hadn't turned into an alien or something.

I had forgotten to take out the contacts. But it was nice to know that even with the blond hair and blue eyes, I still looked enough like me to get asked for an autograph.

"Please," he said, "will you sign a poster?"

I followed him to the tissue and paper products section. There I was greeted by my own smiley face on a cardboard display.

Using Ravi's ballpoint pen, I signed the poster advertising Swan Softie Swabs.

As I handed the pen back, he asked, "Is it true that you raise rats?"

"Actually," I said, "I'm not allowed to have pets. Where did you hear that?"

"Your home page on the internet."

My work history and biography page were posted on the Internet. My agent said I had to do it until I became really, truly famous. But I know it doesn't say anything about rats.

"I don't really remember that much about it. Which page are you talking about?" I answered, wanting him to continue.

"The one on how to become a teenage superstar."

"I think that's a joke," I said. "I'm not a superstar." I should have asked what the address was, but I was too mad to talk more. Inside I was planning on murdering the people who had posted that page. On the outside, I tried to look casual.

I put one foot on the rung of the cart's bottom basket. With my other foot, I pushed away and glided down the aisle. A sudden thought made me skid to a halt. I turned and hollered down the aisle, "Hey, Ravi."

"Yes," he answered.

"Was my telephone number on that home page?"

*****

When we got to the door of Jade's hospital room, Dad went straight down the hall to find Jade's doctor. I

went straight in so that Jade could go straight for the candy bars.

On a normal day she slowly peeled the chocolate outside off, then ate the goo in the middle. She could do that and do it neatly, not getting any stuck to her fingers. Today she bit right into the bar. "Why are you so hungry?" I asked.

"They gave me chipped beef for lunch, and tapioca pudding," she said, sipping a small paper cup of water. "I had fun making sculptures out of them, but that's it. Not that I'm complaining, but I've been dying for some real food."

I tossed a can of soda onto her bed. "Try that."

As she reached for it, her leg moved the covers on the bed slightly. A book with clouds and Indian symbols on the cover peeked from underneath the sheets. I dove for it.

"What's this?" I flipped my thumb across the pages. "Where did you get it?"

"Isn't it neat? I bought it from the hospital gift store. It's on healing powers in nature and explains all about why crystals—Oh!"

She had opened the can of cola, releasing pent up foam all over the sheets. While she was wiping it up with some tissues from a new box Dad had brought her, I noticed her necklace. The pendant hung, pale and pointed, on top of her white pajamas.

"Jade," I said, "it's not like you to believe that necklace can fix you. God is the One who created your entire body so it would heal itself. Besides, I've been reading the Bible straight through. I'm not very far into it, 'cause it's so long, but God didn't like it when all those people made statues and stuff to worship. There's even a little list of rules—God's rules—and rule number one

says not to trust anything more than Him. It's wrong."

"But McKenna," she said, "God made this crystal and maybe even gave it magical powers. I didn't." She picked up the cloud book. "And this book says that the god-force is everywhere and in everything. The spirits of nature can converge and put things straight."

"But Jesus didn't worry about crystals and stuff when He healed people," I said. "He just did it. You told me that. You can pray and talk to God in person. You don't need some rock to help you converge, or purge, or ... whatever."

She put her hand around the crystal and silver charm. I was hoping she would yank it off and throw it away. "It's just that this necklace seems so real," she said, "and God seems so far away. I want something near me when I feel alone."

"But even if you can't see Him," I added, "God is always with you."

"I'm having trouble believing that He is here," she said.

"Why, Jade? You *taught* me that God loves us, no matter what."

"Maybe I was wrong."

"What do you mean, wrong?"

"Where was He when I got caught in the fire, McKenna?" she asked, her eyes blinking and squinting to hold back tears. "And if He was there, why did He let it happen?"

Good question.

Nineteen

I couldn't answer Jade's question, but when I kissed her good-bye, I made sure she was wearing her ID bracelet. "Remember," I said, "you're a daughter of God." If Mom were still alive, she would have been able to say the right things and stay with her, playing cards or working on the crossword. But Dad had work to do, and I had to go with him. I hated leaving my best friend and twin.

As I was walking out the door, the phone rang. Jade picked it up and greeted one of her friends. She had already received a zillion gifts from people at school, and she had the cards and balloons scattered around the room.

If I had been burned, who would send me cards?

*****

As soon as we got home, I headed straight for Dad's computer in the study. After logging onto the internet, I searched for my name. Presto—at least two places.

The first one was a straight biography and résumé with a recent photo, which had been put up by our agent. I had seen that one before. The second page I'd never seen and wasn't sure if I wanted to or not.

It turned out to be no worse than eating soggy cooked carrots. Along with true information about our life, photos from our modeling career came up. There was an accurate history about *Clone Colony* and some publicity photos. *Thoroughbred Fever* as our current job with Galaxy Studios was listed. Everything was fine except for the hobbies section. That's where a photo had been altered. It showed me hugging a huge white rat—and smiling as if I'd just won a zillion dollars.

I found what I was looking for at the bottom of the page. "Want to know more about the James twins?" the home page read. "Call us at (310) 555-1432." There it was, our unlisted, private, home phone number that only family members and a few million of my closest friends could get hold of.

I scrolled back to the top of the page. It had been updated months ago. The World Wide Web address was there all right. It was from our school's newspaper department—and Tasha was the editor.

*****

The next bit of work I had to do was find out about Marcus Harris. I pretended I needed information about him to hire him for a school performance. I called the American Federation of Guards, but they wouldn't give me any of his personal information. Against the rules.

Next, I got out my old call sheets from *Clone Colony.* At the bottom, the phone numbers of the crew were listed. First I would start with Ol' MacDonald.

Mr. MacDonald had been our SAG guardian on the last film, because we didn't have a personal manager then. He was the one who had given us our bracelets and Bibles. He even baptized Jade.

I hoped that he could tell me what to say to Jade to make her give up the crystal stuff. But this time, he wasn't there with all the answers. His answering machine said he was on location for the *Wizard of Oz* project.

Next, I called a few friends from *Clone Colony*'s crew to ask about Marcus and found three people who knew him, two of whom had known him for more than ten years. Marcus's family had been in the movie business forever. I heard enough to tell Mr. Neverland that he had the wrong man. No way would Marcus Harris set those fires.

I made my way back to the computer and logged onto Hollywood On-line, a computer subscription service that carried all the entertainment news. I searched the back issues for details of the other studio fire Mr. Neverland had mentioned. Ashley made it easy for me. She had given a quote to a newspaper reporter, proof she had been on the scenes of all three fires. Ryan had seen her at the set when Jade had been burned, and she'd certainly been there when her own blanket began a blaze.

Last, I called Ryan. I was hoping he would call me first, but I had waited as long I could. When adults won't tell you what's going on, it's all the more important to find out what it is—and fast. The only person under twenty who might know why Mrs. Kennett left in the middle of her job was my ex-almost-boyfriend, Ryan Kennett.

*****

I called the house. After the third ring a familiar voice answered, "Kennetts' residence."

What is Tasha doing at Ryan's house?

"Hi, Tasha," I said.

She noticed the North Pole frost in my tone, because she said, "McKenna, what's wrong?"

"Oh, nothing," I answered. "I was just calling to tell Ryan that if he ever loses my phone number, he can find it on the internet."

The reference to the home page her newspaper staff had created caught Tasha off guard. There was complete silence on her side of the line. Finally she said, "Ryan can't come to the phone, McKenna. May I take a message and have him call you back?"

Who does she think she is? His secretary or something?

"No, you may not take a message," I said. "Either you can get Ryan, or you can tell me why you put up the picture of the rat and my phone number. Your choice."

"Actually," she said, "I have a third option." The dial tone told me what it was. She had hung up.

*****

"Dad," I said, interrupting him while he watched an eleven o'clock news show, "if Jade is well enough, can we go to church on Sunday?" I knew I would need support to get Jade thinking about God again.

"I was wondering when one of you was going to ask that." He clicked off the TV and leaned back on the black leather couch in the den.

I sat next to him. "Did you and Mom ever go to church together?" I asked.

"Sure we did, but I just went along for the ride. I wish now that I had paid a bit more attention. . . . Where would you like to go? There's that glass church overlooking the ocean—"

"Where did you and Mom go?"

"That one is too far away. It's over an hour's drive."

"What was the name of it?" I asked.

"Burbank Faith Presbyterian."

"What's a Pres . . . whatchamacallit."

"I don't know. I told you I didn't pay attention. But I tell you what, one of my golf buddies goes to a big church near here. I'll ask him what time the services are."

I guessed one church was as good as another. At least Jade and I could learn more about God. I stood up to leave.

"Before you go, McKenna," he said, "I talked to Mrs. Kennett on my cell phone just a few minutes ago. She said I could tell you."

She's got cancer? She's getting a divorce? She's quitting?

"She had to leave the studio this afternoon because Ryan got suspended from school."

Ryan?

"What for?" I asked, not really wanting to know.

"He set off an explosion in the chemistry room. If the school charges him with criminal conduct, he may have to go to jail."

Twenty

I hate the radio when adults have control of it.

I especially hate it when the radio plays old-fashioned love songs while the guy you used to like is sitting next to you in a car, but you can't talk because his mom is driving. I tried to block out the music and rehearse my lines silently, but the song must have lulled me to sleep. I didn't realize I'd dozed off on the way to the racetrack where we would film Thunderbolt's victory scenes. Ryan tugged on my shirtsleeve.

"Wake up, McKenna, we're here," he said, and shoved a tissue into my hand. "You were drooling. Use this."

I do not drool. But I decided to take the tissue, just in case. As I reached for it, my hand accidentally brushed his.

"What?" he asked. He must have thought the touch was a signal or something.

First things first. I wiped off my mouth with the tissue, but it felt dry. Then I answered his question. "Nothing." I guess I really didn't want to speak to him, even though I wanted to know about the chemistry fire—and about Tasha. But it was none of my business.

If he wanted to blow up the world and marry Tasha, that was fine with me. I didn't care. Really.

"Why did you call yesterday?" He glanced to make sure his mom was out of gossip range, and then he whispered, "Even though I'm on restriction, I tried calling you back, but the line was busy for over an hour. Well, then Mom came back. . . ."

"It was nothing really. Tasha cleared up everything."

"Right," he said, obviously not believing me. He shoved open the car door.

We both got out. After looking in the car's side mirrors and checking for spittle again, I found nothing. I bunched up the tissue and threw it at him. "You liar. I did not drool."

The wad hit his ear, and he pretended to be fatally wounded in the head. As he pressed both palms flat against his ears and shouted, "She got me!" he also staggered backward.

"Ryan," his mother interrupted the scene, "stop the theatrics. You're in enough trouble already. Don't add to it."

Ryan scowled, but the minilecture worked because he calmed down. We left the restricted parking area and headed toward the crowd outside the racetrack.

*****

Ryan was an extra for the day, because, according to Mr. Harley, he wasn't welcome at school, and, according to his mother, he wasn't to be trusted at home alone.

Extras don't have speaking parts in movies. They mostly just stand around. In this case, Ryan and the thousand others would be sitting in stands, cheering at

an imaginary horse race.

Mrs. Kennett asked me to wait for her while she got breakfast at the caterer's trailer. Ryan said good-bye, and I watched him walk away toward the signs that said, "EXTRAS CHECK IN HERE." An arrow on the sign pointed behind the grandstands. Yellow and white flags flew above the risers, and landscapers were still adding the final touches to the set, planting flowers and trimming bushes.

Ryan passed behind a small man in an olive-green jumpsuit who was digging holes for marigolds. Ryan looked over his shoulder at me to see if I was watching, and then pretended to kick the man in the rear end. Just then, the man stood up, and his mustached face turned in our direction. Ryan stopped in midkick, his black basketball shoe hanging in the air. He couldn't hold the one-footed stance and tumbled backward.

As Ryan landed in the freshly turned dirt, I laughed and then rushed over to help him. I grabbed his hand to pull him up. But instead of rising, he held mine tight and pulled me down with him.

"You do care," he said playfully, his face close to mine. "I was wondering when you'd be nice to me again." His lashes were charcoal black, and his eyes green as the forest. But I looked away from them in an instant.

"I'm always nice," I said, yanking my hand away and leaning back. "I was just being a friend."

"For once," he said.

"What's that supposed to mean?"

"You don't seem to have many friends at school," Ryan announced. "In fact, if it weren't for Jade's friends, like Tasha, I doubt you'd have a single one. Except for . . ."

Except for you. He didn't have to say the last words.

I'd had enough crank phone calls to know it was true.

"And I'm beginning to think Tasha's right," Ryan continued. "Ever since you hit the 'big time,' you are too moody."

"You'd be moody too if you had to work for Mr. Knighton," I snapped, "and your sister was almost burned up, and your dad was being sued." I didn't mention that Jade wanted to worship a rock, and a supposed friend had put my phone number on the internet. But I should have, because I wanted him to feel sorry for me, and instead of giving me sympathy, he said,

"Well, I'm not letting it get to me that I've been kicked out of school, grounded till I'm twenty-one, and could face criminal charges. You don't hear me saying it's all *your* fault."

"*My* fault?"

"Yeah," Ryan said as if I should have known it all along. "I was trying to figure out how someone could set a fire like the one that got Jade. My lab partners and I were getting pretty close to figuring it out. We had a book on making fireworks from ordinary chemicals. One of the guys accidentally spilled something, and before we knew it. . . ."

I put one hand on the ground to push myself up, and it landed on a wire half-buried in soil. *Must be some weird way to hold up the plants.* I looked around for the little man who had been digging, but he was gone. His red toolbox, some wire, and some perky gold flowers were left.

"Hey," I said to Ryan, "that guy forgot all his stuff."

"You must have scared him off." He stood up, shoving his hands in his jeans pockets. "You're good at that." He left, following the signs posted for extras, and this time he didn't look back.

*****

After yesterday's costume blowup, I bet LaShondra was worried about losing her job. She jittered and bounced twice as much as usual. Due to her efforts, I was on the set in the proper clothes a half hour early.

"Stay put!" she said.

"I'm not the one who disappears," I said.

She actually stopped bouncing for a minute and looked me in the eye. "Let me tell you something, girl. I'm here to help you, but you've got to look after yourself. No one's going to do it for you. If you can't find me, check with an AD to find out what's going on. You've got to be a survivor. You can't last in this business unless you're tough."

"How's the headache?" I asked.

She didn't answer, but just shook her head. The look in her eye told me Snap had been right about the migraine.

"I have to find Chantella," she said as she walked away. Chantella DuBois played Aunt Savannah and had won best actress two years ago. Everyone was saying that, with this movie, she had a good shot at winning again. Rand Knighton played Uncle Fredrick, her husband, and so the movie had definite box office draw. Even if no one on earth saw *Clone Colony*, I would have a place in Hollywood history for acting in *Thoroughbred Fever*.

Being with such a famous cast made missing the remake of *The Wizard of Oz* almost bearable. If you didn't count boy troubles, because those never go away, I should have been totally happy. But there was Jade to consider. The fact that my sister was in the hospital

spoiled my fun. She was missing out, and I had a hollow space in my stomach whenever I thought about her. The ache would go away if I could find out who was setting those fires.

How can I find out if Ashley set them? She was at all three locations when they happened. The only thing I need to know is why she would do it. And proof. I need proof.

Twenty-one

Have you ever noticed that everything seems to go just fine right before life falls apart? Like your favorite song comes on the radio, and then your dad decides to listen to a football game. Or you think you have an A in a class, and then your teacher checks her math. She tells you she figured it wrong, that you really have a C-.

The filming was like that. The short and sugary sweet rehearsal with Rand Knighton and Chantella DuBois went great. The cameras got their lines and smiles with me saying my yes ma'ams and sirs. The waiter served and poured at the right cues. A simple, charming scene for the opening of the big race.

Chantella, thin as dental floss, looked willowy in a pale green dress. Mr. Knighton, even though he was Dad's age, was hard not to watch. His dark suit and white shirt made his hair and tan glow. He looked half swanky lawyer, half Tarzan.

There were no temper tantrums. Nobody was fired. The root beer Mr. Knighton wanted ebbed and flowed whenever he asked it to.

A happy day.

Memories of the fire, of lawsuits, and of crystal necklaces vanished.

Mrs. Kennett and the crowd of crew and other onlookers sat in white plastic chairs behind the camera cranes and sound equipment.

In the grandstands, Ms. Haveshire was milling about with the extras, making sure they sat in the correct places and the stands were filled evenly. The assistant director yelled orders through a bullhorn and told them when to cheer or boo. It was a lot of work for the background of a scene.

After we were done filming, Chantella said to me, "You've got it—whatever it is they're looking for." She put her delicate fingers underneath my chin and moved my head from side to side, studying every pore. "Does your sister have the exact same bone structure?"

I nodded.

"What about the perfect skin? And the little mole beside your left eye?"

I nodded again.

"Incredible," she said. "When I was your age I had a face full of pimples and a double chin." She dropped her hand.

I tried to imagine her anything except perfect. I knew a lot of my dad's clients chose the likeness of her nose when they had plastic surgery. And once I had tried to pluck my eyebrows to look like hers, but after four or five tweezes, I had had enough of beauty pain and left the thick hairs alone.

"I'm going to look out for you, McKenna," she said.

My heart practically stopped when I heard her words. I hardly had any friends, and here was a Hollywood great telling me she was going to help my career.

Chantella continued, "I don't want you crushed like some of the pretty flowers I've seen trampled in

Hollywood. You stick by me for this filming, and I'll teach you some tricks."

LaShondra, however, had ideas on ways to unstick us. She walked over, clipboard on her hip. "McKenna, it's time for you to go to tutoring. We've got to squeeze in your three hours of school. They're only filming the crowd now."

I wanted to stay with Chantella. "Let's blow it off for today," I said. "I'll do extra work tomorrow."

Chantella, steel underneath silk, put her hand on my arm and pushed me away. "Go on and get an education. There's nothing more annoying than a stupid woman."

I certainly didn't want to be annoying, especially to Chantella. I walked toward the school trailer to wake up old Mrs. Bixby, the onetime dancer.

*****

Mrs. Bixby wasn't asleep when I got to the classroom. She was sitting in a chair, which she more than filled, and reading a book. On the cover, a pretty woman wearing a ripped dress and a man with a naked chest embraced each other. They looked as if they were at the end of a school dance. Those romance books always made me wonder if grown-ups acted any differently than high school couples did.

We had settled into a nice routine, Mrs. Bixby and I. I worked on my stuff, she read her romance. Neither one wanted any interruptions, so it was quiet enough for me to hear the applause and cheers of the extras outside.

After about fifteen minutes, I also heard the explosions. I didn't wait around to see if they disturbed Mrs. Bixby. In seconds, I shoved away from the desk, left the

school trailer, and followed the sound of the screams.

Fire blazed in the roofs above the stands. I looked at the owners' box to see if Chantella was OK, but the set was gone, exploded to sticks and splinters.

O God, what am I supposed to do? I prayed.

For a good five seconds, I stood numb. People ran down the riser steps, and the yellow and white flags surrounding the racetrack waved cheerfully despite the fire burning them up.

I was jolted to action by Thunderbolt's massive chest and clomping hooves rushing past me. The black horse was followed by my friend, the horse wrangler.

"Hey," I called to him, ashamed of myself for never finding out his name, "what's going on?"

"Bombs," he hollered over his shoulder. *"Arriba."*

"Hurry," he had said in Spanish. *Hurry and do what?*

*****

The air crackled with the sound of dry wood burning. The smoke rose gray and thick even though there were no winds to lift it up and away. I thanked God that none of the six stairways to the stands was destroyed. The extras shoved their way down the stairs, past the flower beds, running to the center of the racetrack, a green oasis with no burning boards above it.

It looked as if the bombs had been set off at the far end and rear of the grandstands, on seats that had been empty all day. The explosions had blasted away from the crowds, and none of the seats were really destroyed. The fires at the top of the stands must have been started separately. All in all, it didn't seem like a war zone or anything. The extras hadn't trampled each other. The AD was directing everyone to the nearest set

of stairs with the bullhorn.

"Keep to the right . . . you there in the red shirt. Go to your left—"

Another attention getter? Explosions with no casualties. Fires above the stands, not in them.

I looked around for news crews. None. I ran over to one of the cameramen and asked if anyone had been in the owners' box. "No one, I hope," he answered as he rolled his camera away. "I was shooting the extras in the stands. All the set carpenters and most of the light crew were setting up outside of the stables."

"What about Chantella and Mr. Knighton?" I asked. "Where are they?"

"Kid, how would I know? Can't you see a fire is going on?"

I could. Not knowing what else to do, I stood directly in front of the stands, breathed the smoke, and heard the loud crack of splitting wood. One support beam for the stand's covering snapped and began to fall. So much for a "safe" fire. The long, thick piece of lumber plunged toward about forty people who were still pushing their way down the narrow stairways. Three dozen mothers, fathers, sons, or daughters in the way of falling, flaming wood.

I had to do something, anything, useful or not. So I started screaming with the rest of the crowd. "Look out!" I yelled, running toward the stands as the beam fell into the crowd.

"Everyone move left, move left!" shouted the AD through his bullhorn.

"McKenna!" a voice cried over all the other sounds.

I turned and found Marcus Harris. He was holding a red toolbox.

Twenty-two

I stared at the toolbox. A piece of wire was sticking out of one side, as if it were a snake dangling its poisonous head from a tree. A bomb detonation wire?

My hands started to shake as my emotions battled with my brain.

He didn't set the fires or the explosions. Marcus cares about people, said my heart.

Then why is he holding that toolbox? Why has he been at all the fires? said my brain.

"McKenna?" he grabbed my hand with his free one. "Is everything OK?"

I shook my head and pointed at the fallen overhang.

"Oh no. Not that." His boyish face turned pale as ash. "She said no one would get hurt—" And with that he ran toward the stands. The adrenaline speeding up my heart pushed me to follow him.

*****

We weren't the only ones who had seen the danger and rushed to give aid. The entire roof structure had collapsed, bending almost to the ground. Three smoldering sections had fallen, hitting about five people who didn't

make it out of the grandstands. The first victim we came to was caught underneath a beam. He was just on the other side of the flower bed, on the first seats of the grandstands. I recognized him as a light technician; he wore jeans and a blue polo shirt and was pinned by the legs. A woman was next to him, free, but unconscious.

She lay on her back, eyes closed, chin tilted up. She looked dressed for a funeral in her black dress. Marcus put down the box and helped the grip move the beam. The trapped man pushed as Marcus heaved the wood off of him. "She was on the ground before the beam broke," the grip said, rubbing his thigh. "I was trying to get her away from the smoke when it fell. . . . I'll go see if anyone else needs help." He limped off.

Marcus knelt beside the silvery blond woman and pinched her upturned nose shut with one hand. His other rested on her chin. He was giving her the kiss of life—mouth-to-mouth resuscitation.

O God, please don't let this kiss be her last.

Marcus forced her lungs to work with long, slow breaths. I watched as the woman's very life was being given by the man who might have tried to take it away. Marcus' voice softly spoke to her, trying to make emotional contact.

As soon as her chest began to rise and fall on its own, I silently gave God a prayer of thanks. Quickly picking up the toolbox while Marcus was still paying attention to the patient, I pushed through the small crowd that had gathered around us.

Suddenly, the siren of a fire engine pierced through the noise.

That grating wail has got to be the most beautiful sound in the world.

I knew I had to find Ryan—and Mrs. Kennett. I also

needed to hide the toolbox. It could have the proof against Ashley I needed. Hadn't Marcus said, "*She* said no one would get hurt"?

*****

The fire was out, doused by eight hoses and twice as many firefighters by the time I found the Kennetts waiting in the station wagon. Ryan had his body stuck halfway out the window. He waved his arm to get my attention.

"McKenna," he yelled, "tell my mom I didn't blow up the set!"

He had probably been near the fire's start, but Mrs. Kennett could have been anywhere. "Where were you when it happened?" I asked her.

"I was in your dressing room, lying down," she said. "I needed to do something about a headache." By the looks of her, the puffy skin under the eyes, and the gray tint to her skin, she was going to have a headache for a long time to come. Apparently, headaches were common in this business.

Ryan looked the same, just a bit rumpled.

"Are you all right?" I asked him.

"Yes, I was in the stands when the first explosion went off," he explained. "At first I thought it was just some loud noise from the movie equipment or something. I jumped over the railing yelling, 'Air raid!' "

Why do I believe that?

"I thought maybe I could get a job as a stuntman if Ms. Haveshire saw me," he said. "Good thing, because I was one of the first out of the stands. I saw the fire race around the top of the stands and the explosions at the base of the stands go off. I ran to help let the horses out

of the stables, just in case the fire spread there. Animals go crazy when there's fire around."

So that's why Thunderbolt was running free.

"How did you find your mom?"

"I was looking for you, so I checked in your trailer. Mom was there instead, and she made me come to the car." He paused, trying hard not to let his disappointment show. "I didn't even get anywhere near the fire-fighters."

Mrs. Kennett asked, "McKenna, will they let us go home now? You don't think they'll want you to work under these circumstances?"

"We can't go," I said. "Not until I make sure everyone is OK. I also need my clothes and personal things back. Who knows if the police will let people in later."

"Mom, can we please go?" Ryan pleaded. "You can come with us." He held his hands in an exaggerated gesture of begging, fingers clasped just underneath his chin.

"Oh, all right. Fifteen minutes." She didn't have the heart to fight him or the energy to accompany us. She let us go just so she could have some peace.

I waited until he was out of the car, and we were both out of his mom's earshot. "You didn't see Ashley anywhere did you?" I asked.

"That blond girl?" he said.

"Yeah." I said, hoping for a yes. I wanted her to be guilty, guilty, guilty.

"As a matter of fact, I didn't," he said.

I didn't bother showing my disappointment, and I didn't bother telling him about the toolbox. If Ashley were part of the bombing, maybe she had the brains to wear a disguise this time.

We walked a few steps before we got to the entrance.

I asked, "So . . . why was Tasha over at your house when I called?"

"Don't you know?"

"Would I be asking if I did?"

"Tasha," Ryan said, "sometimes baby-sits after school gets out if I have stuff after school. She watches my younger brothers even more often now that Mom is working as your 'personal manager.' " He made "personal manager" sound snobby. "We're hardly ever there at the same time," he said, "just in case your nosey little brain was wondering about that. I just happened to be home early yesterday 'cause Mr. Harley decided I wasn't wanted at school for a week."

What could I say? He couldn't help whom his mother chose to watch the kids.

"Do you finally believe that I don't like Tasha?" he asked. "Or do you have any more questions?"

Just one: Why am I so stupid?

Twenty-three

Ryan and I walked through the gate, back into the land of cinders, sobbing, and security guards. The officer keeping spectators out recognized me, letting Ryan and me pass through together. I headed in the general direction of the ambulances parked on the racetrack. Ryan followed closely behind through a thick crowd of people preparing to leave. We waited while several people tried to get out the narrow chain-link opening.

"There's McKenna James!" a woman squealed, pointing at me.

Suddenly, we were at the center of a large crowd of extras, and I was signing autographs on anything available: dollar bills, grocery receipts, tissues.

"Are you all right?" an elderly man in a bright Hawaiian shirt asked me. Before I could answer, smile, and make excuses to get away, the squealing woman noticed Ryan.

"Hey," she said, "you with the brown hair. Aren't you the one who leaped over the railing?"

"Yeah," said another voice, "he's the only one who got out of the stands before the fire started. He knew the place was going to blow up!"

One more woman spoke up, "I saw him turn the

horses loose. He's done everything he can to ruin this movie." Looking at Ryan and pointing a finger at his face, she said, "What are you, some sort of animal rights advocate who's protesting horse racing?"

The crowd, hot and smoke-stained, pulled in tight around us. The bodies breathed in unison. And they were all out to get Ryan.

"Hey!" I said in a loud voice. "He always does that—jumps over fences and stuff." Everyone was listening to me, so I added, "He's practicing to be a stuntman." The crowd laughed, but not very nicely. I felt someone gently squeeze my shoulder. I turned to find Mr. Neverland.

"Let me handle this," he whispered. He left my side and positioned himself a little to Ryan's right. He took out his badge and flashed it to the crowd.

"Hello everybody," he yelled. "I'm Investigator Neverland. No need to worry about this young man." He slapped Ryan on the back. "We've already arrested someone else and received a full confession. We'll make an announcement to the press just as soon as my colleagues are finished searching for physical evidence to verify the statement."

He took Ryan's arm and led him out of harm's way. Easing my way out of the crowd too, I caught up with them. "Thanks," Ryan was saying to Mr. Neverland when we were several paces away. "I don't think I could have dodged them all if I had to make a run for it."

"People who have been traumatized are hotheaded," Mr. Neverland said with a smile. He stopped walking, and we formed a little huddle. "One time I went inside the basement of a burning apartment building. I was just doing my job, looking for evidence. I came out with a can of gasoline, and the mob of renters was convinced I was the arsonist. My badge meant nothing. Lucky for

me, an officer drove by in a patrol car. He probably saved my life. I thought they were going to throw me back inside." He chuckled to himself, happy with the memory.

Ryan and I laughed too; we relaxed for the first time since the first explosion. Then I remembered what the investigator had said to the crowd. "Mr. Neverland, did someone really confess?" I asked.

"As soon as we showed Marcus Harris some of the debris from the explosives, he cracked," Mr. Neverland explained. "He took responsibility for all the fires, even the one on the other set. I think the confession was good for him. He couldn't wait to tell us he did it."

I shook my head. "But he isn't that kind of person. He *cares* about people. I watched him save a woman. He'd do *anything* to help someone."

Mr. Neverland put his arm around me. "I know you didn't want it to be him."

"But listen," I said, "all his friends said he was happy. He had been a child actor, he had all the attention he wanted, and *he gave it up*. He wouldn't have done it."

"McKenna, the guy already confessed," Ryan said, trying to help. "What do you want Mr. Neverland to do?"

"But what about the man with the wire we saw this morning? He was planting more than flowers. He was planting bombs!"

Ryan gave Mr. Neverland a wink. "Yeah, sure he was. Maybe he put a little too much fertilizer on 'em."

Not even Mr. Neverland believed me. "Well," he said, "if we have time, we'll look for your man, McKenna. But Marcus told us how he did it all alone, and that he had access to the explosives and stole the stuff from Al's assistant."

I should have told them about the red toolbox right then. But the anger I felt at not being believed kept me quiet. The knowledge gave me a secret power. *I'll show the toolbox to someone who'll believe me. Then we'll see who really set those fires. No one would treat Nancy Drew this way.*

Mr. Neverland gave my shoulders an understanding squeeze. "You would have felt a lot better if it had been Ashley or someone you didn't like. But it's for the best. Marcus will get help, and at least you know that there will be no more fires."

*****

At home, leaning back on three pillows and painting her nails, Jade listened to my version of the fire and explosions. My twin was still wearing her crystal necklace, and her Bible was underneath the cloud book on the table next to the bed. But I didn't bring up the subject of the New Age. I hadn't had a chance to read more in my Bible, and until I got to the end, I wasn't sure if I would know what to say.

I also didn't want her too worried to go back to the set on Monday, so I didn't mention Ashley or the red toolbox. Instead, I told her about Ryan and Tasha.

"I don't get it," she said. "You're mad at Tasha because she took a baby-sitting job?"

"Well, it was at Ryan's house...."

Jade patiently finished dabbing her thumbnail with the polish, then she blew on it. She held her hand away from her face and evaluated the paint job.

I admit when Jade started to question me, the charges against Tasha sounded weak. Tasha didn't stay up at night thinking of ways to make me mad. But she

119

had been rude to me when I talked to her on the phone the other day.

"What about hanging up on me?" I had a right to gripe about that.

"You would have done the same thing." Jade started painting her other hand. She held the brush with two stiff, straight fingers, the others fanned out so as not to smudge the fresh paint. "Face it, McKenna," she said, beginning to paint her pinkie, "Tasha's just a little too much like you."

I stood up and began to pace her bedroom. "What about the home page on the Web with our pictures?"

"Have you asked her about it?" Jade said. "I mean, maybe she didn't have a thing to do with it. There are several people who work on the school newspaper, you know."

I decided to let the subject drop. Ryan was right. I really didn't have any friends besides Jade. And maybe him, if a guy can ever be a friend.

"Jade," I said, "should I ask Ryan to go with us to the premiere showing of *Clone Colony?*"

"I can't answer that. You've got to get in touch with your inner consciousness and do what you feel is right."

God, I prayed silently, *will I ever get my sister back?*

Twenty-four

The next morning, we went to church together. It was the first time we'd ever been to a church when it wasn't a Christmas service. Without a bunch of red poinsettias and white-and-gold angels, a church looks rather colorless. This new church was OK. The building didn't have those hard benches or stained-glass windows as older ones usually do. The chairs were beige, padded, and somewhat soft. Comfortable enough, anyway, for Dad to settle in and listen to the preacher's speech. I listened and understood pretty much. But it didn't seem to do anything for Jade. She didn't burst into tears and denounce her crystal necklace.

One interesting thing happened when they passed around a brass dish during a song. Jade jabbed me in the side with her elbow. "McKenna," she whispered, "look over there." She pointed down near the front. The short pastor who had visited her in the hospital was collecting the bowls of money at a table down in front. "That man came and talked to me my first day in the hospital," she said.

"What did he say?" I asked, curious now to find out what had happened but unwilling to tell my part in it.

"I don't remember much, because the pain medica-

tion for the burn made me drowsy," she said.

"Did he pray or something?" I pictured him standing straight as a pine, sucking in his stomach and uttering something meaningful. Maybe reading some important part of the Bible with one hand raised.

"No," she said.

"What did he do?"

"I don't know. I fell asleep," she said. "I never mentioned it because I thought it was a dream. But that's the guy. I remember his tie. Who would wear a tie with tombstones on it to a hospital?"

*****

On Monday, Dad inspected Jade's burn. He poked and squinted a lot. But it must have been healing OK because he said Jade could spend a half day at the studio.

"Since they've caught the arsonist," Dad said, "I suppose it's safe enough." We had to promise to change her gauze bandage and check for any signs of infection. We had to promise to wash it and apply some special goop. We had to promise not to tire her out, to rest, to eat right, to be good, and to stay out of trouble.

Mrs. Kennett dropped us off at the front door of the studio and went to park the car. There were no empty spaces near the front door, and with everyone so worried about her, Jade couldn't be expected to walk that far.

When we walked in the building, a few members of the crew gave us double takes. Since Jade didn't stay on the set long that first day, many didn't know that I was an identical twin. We passed the stares and the dressing rooms to find LaShondra first thing. The talent coordi-

nator got off the phone and shook Jade's hand. "You're not McKenna, right?" LaShondra asked, her black braids dancing. She reminded me of a bird, the way her head was always moving.

My sister nodded.

"Since you've been gone," the talent coordinator said, "let's get you to makeup and out to the set. And you, McKenna—"

"Will have to go to school," I finished for her. "I'm going. I'm going."

$$\star\star\star\star\star$$

I was only a half hour into my math when Jade came through the classroom door wearing her own clothes.

"I've . . . been . . . fired!" she wailed. At least that's what I think she said. It was hard to tell because of all the sobs in between each word. She sank down into a chair.

"Join the club," Mrs. Bixby said from her chair in the corner. "There aren't too many in Hollywood who haven't been fired one time or another."

Jade's breathing gradually got smoother. She was almost calm when I said, "It'll be OK."

"No it won't," she said. "He threw me out. He said to never come back. They made me change out of my wardrobe clothes."

"Oh, Lord," exhaled Mrs. Bixby, struggling to get out of her chair. She made it and walked over to Jade to give comfort.

"Don't talk about God," snapped Jade. "If He loved me, none of this would have happened." Mrs. Bixby took a step back when she heard the anger in Jade's voice.

Just then LaShondra burst in. She ignored my sobbing sister.

"Good!" she said in triumph. "You're here, McKenna. Get to makeup. Scat. Knighton wants you." She grabbed me by the forearm and pulled me to the door.

I shot Jade a look that said I was sorry, and I was off to face the dragon.

*****

Snap had a tiny part in the scene, and he and LaShondra were waiting for me when I came out of my dressing room.

"What happened?" I asked him. "What did Jade do?"

"Nothing, really." He ran his fingers through his hair and shook his head. "It's just that she's not *you*. Knighton can tell the difference in your personalities, and he didn't like it. This sharing a role thing isn't going to work, even if it does speed up production."

"Was he a total monster?"

"Yeah," he said.

I noticed he didn't give any details and guessed it was probably really bad. Poor Jade. When Claude the hair stylist had warned me about the director liking one of us and hating the other, I always assumed he would like Jade. Everyone *always* likes her best. If it caused my sister so much pain, I didn't know if I liked this popularity.

But I didn't worry about it long just then. LaShondra shoved me onto the set. Rand and I were the main actors working in the scene. He had rewritten some lines, so I had to read my cues from a TelePrompTer, a TV right above the camera that displays the script.

A few of the crew were new. I wondered if some had

quit because of yesterday's bombs. Dad's *Los Angeles Times* had reported that no one died and that only seven people had to go to the hospital.

But the people here were focused on today, this moment. They all acted as if they'd forgotten about Jade. The filming went smoothly. I even had to admire the way Rand worked as actor and director. If he didn't like what was happening, he'd tell the director of photography, and we'd do the scene again. Sometimes, I thought he was being too picky, or just wanted to waste time. But I have to admit, most of his changes were for the best. Whatever else Mr. Knighton might be, the man could create a great film.

As Snap and I left the set, he asked if I'd seen Ms. Haveshire.

"No. Why?"

"She was looking for you right after Jade, uh, left."

Twenty-five

It was time to check Jade's bandage. Then I figured we had about a half hour to look for the red toolbox before the end of lunch. We could sneak in at the end of the line and hope that all the salads were gone. Then we'd have to eat two desserts each to make sure we had enough energy.

Inside the classroom, Mrs. Bixby was halfway through a novel; Jade's science book was open; her chair was pushed back, but my twin wasn't there.

"Oh, hello," Mrs. Bixby said after I coughed to get her attention.

"Where's my sister?"

"She went somewhere with Marti Haveshire. . . ." She leaned forward to gossip, her eyes and mouth wide open. "I don't know why that woman came back to the set after the news about her son. I wouldn't be able to show my face if that had happened to me."

"What happened?" I asked.

"You know, Marcus confessed to the explosions."

It surprised me that Mrs. Bixby had picked up information that I didn't know. I would be surprised if she did anything except read novels and eat. "I heard about his confession," I said patiently. "What has Marcus got

to do with Ms. Haveshire?"

"Oh, honey," the woman said, "she's his mother. She's been planning his acting career since he was a baby. It broke her heart when he went into firefighting. And now this."

"But their last names aren't the same . . ."

Even before I'd finished speaking, I knew the answer. Remarriage.

"That Marti has been married at least four times," she said. "The last one was to an actor ten years younger than she is!"

Ms. Haveshire and Marcus. Everyone in Hollywood is related to somebody.

"Well, that is bad news. I'd like to go tell her how sorry I am," I said, while a plan was forming in my head. "Did Ms. Haveshire mention where she was taking Jade?"

"Now, I don't know you well enough to play your little game," she laughed, her double chins wobbling. "I admit, I don't know if you're McKenna or Jade. You're as exact as two plain marshmallows. But Ms. Haveshire called her McKenna, and the girl didn't object."

That's Jade all right. She never corrects people because she doesn't want to hurt their feelings.

"Marti said," Mrs. Bixby finished, "that she needed help finding a red toolbox. Mc—your sister volunteered to help her look for it."

*****

It's a good thing I didn't have lunch, because I would have gotten an upset stomach when I jumped up and down for joy. *Ms. Haveshire is looking for evidence that will help prove her son didn't do it! Marcus must have*

told her to look for the red toolbox. It might be evidence that he's innocent. She'll believe me and help me convince the others!

I ran to find Thunderbolt's caretaker. The day before, I had left the toolbox with him, asking him to hide it as the favor he said he owed me. As I wound my way through the horse trailers looking for him, I found Ms. Haveshire first. She was pacing near the parking lot, smoking a cigarette, as if waiting for something or someone important.

"Where's Jade?" I said. My question startled her. She jumped back a little, her mouth hanging open and smoke wafting out. Her eye shadow matched the ashes at the end of the cigarette. When she inhaled on the white stick, I couldn't help but notice her mouth. The red mark above her lip was still there, red and blotchy.

"Jade? You're *both* here today?" Ms. Haveshire said, sounding confused. She had gotten us mixed up, just as Mrs. Bixby had said.

"Yes," I said. "Did you find the toolbox? I can help you. But first I need to find Jade. I promised Dad I'd look out for her."

Plus, I wanted her to help catch the real arsonist. That might help her feel better after being kicked off the set.

Ms. Haveshire laughed a little. "I'll be glad to take you to her. She insisted on seeing Thunderbolt. And I wanted a cigarette, so I came back outside. . . . But just for the record," she said, "where did you hide the toolbox?"

"I don't know where it is. But I gave it to Thunderbolt's groom. He said he'd take good care of it."

"I see," Ms. Haveshire said as we walked to the trailer.

"I want the same thing you do," I told her.

"And what exactly is that?" she asked carefully.

"I want to see Marcus go free," I said, "and help trap the real arsonist. With that toolbox, we can catch the man who did it. I saw him burying the bombs or wires or something. His fingerprints are probably all over it."

"I want that toolbox too," she said and got out a new cigarette.

We turned the corner of Studio 30 and walked toward an aluminum trailer far away from the others. I heard Jade before I could see her. "Let me out!" she was yelling in between pounds on the side of the trailer door.

"Good thing we came back," said Ms. Haveshire. "You can't open the doors from the inside. No one wants the horse to accidentally get out. Here, let me get the door."

"It's OK, Jade," I yelled, as Ms. Haveshire lifted the heavy metal latch. "I'm here. We'll let you out." I was too worried about getting her out to wonder how she'd gotten locked in.

"McKenna?" she called, then started coughing. "Who is 'we'?"

Before I could answer, Ms. Haveshire opened the door a crack. I pushed past her shoulder to step inside. "Be my guest," Ms. Haveshire said and opened the door wider. I felt a shove on the small of my back and stumbled headfirst into the trailer. "No!" Jade screamed the instant I felt the blow to the side of my head.

Before I blacked out, I heard Ms. Haveshire slam the door and yell, "You're the only one who knows about that toolbox. And its secret is going to die with you."

Twenty-six

I woke to the smell of smoke mingled with horse manure.

"God, Oh God," Jade was saying. "Please, wake up my sister. Please get us out of here. Please help me put these fires out."

As I struggled to sit up, I saw the hooves. They were attached to black legs. Horse legs. And they weren't still; they were pawing at the sawdust on the floor. Dry, burning sawdust.

"Put it out," I said to Jade. "Why are you just standing there?"

"I can't get to it," she said. "The horse, I don't want to let him out."

There was a gate across the trailer keeping Thunderbolt and the fire, at least for now, at the far end. Ryan had been right. Horses do go crazy when there's fire around.

I raised my hand to stroke his nose. "Good boy, Charlie," I used his real name and cooed in a fake Spanish accent.

Instead of calming down, he backed and then reared.

In those seconds, Jade got close enough to grab the handle of the water pail that was hanging in

Thunderbolt's section. Lifting the metal bucket off a hook, she brought the bucket back behind her, then heaved the water toward the flames.

The spit and sizzle of quenched flames was short-lived. After an initial hissing, the fire roared higher. That's when I smelled the gasoline.

"How did this start?" I asked Jade.

"Ms. Haveshire threw her cigarette in the back corner."

"Why didn't you push out before she closed the door?"

"I was making sure you weren't dead," she said. "You did get hit on the head."

"Did she hit me?"

"No, I did it." Her cheeks flushed red. It could have been due to the heat of the fire or to embarrassment. "I thought Ms. Haveshire was coming in. I swung the metal divider, and it hit you in the head."

"Stay low so you don't breathe the smoke," I said. "I've got an idea." I crossed into Thunderbolt's section, moving slowly and hoping horses don't like to bite.

"It's all right," I said as I slid the blanket off his back and started to smother the flames with it. I stopped when I felt the heat on my hand. The blanket had caught fire.

I looked around for something else to use against the fire. There was a narrow door at the end of the trailer I hadn't seen before. I threw the smoldering blanket down right in front of it, stepped on the blanket and opened the door. Inside were three saddles on special racks, leather harnesses, and a heavy woolen blanket. Thinking it might last longer than the cotton horse cover, I grabbed the blanket. Underneath lay the red toolbox.

Jade started to scream again through one of the three tiny windows near the top of the trailer. Even if we could squeeze out the opening, we didn't have time to pry off the bars. I'd never noticed how much a horse trailer is like a prison cell. Small and cramped, tiny barred windows, and a door that can only be opened from the outside.

"Help! Fire!" Jade screamed, and kicked at the door. "Fire! Fire!"

Maybe everyone else isn't at lunch. Maybe someone will hear. But let's not count on it.

"Jade," I said, "grab his halter. I found the toolbox. I need room to haul it out. Maybe there's a hammer or something we can use."

Jade grabbed the nylon halter tightly; she pulled so that the horse moved a bit. He was still freaked by the fire and reared, but Jade hung on.

The fire, no longer satisfied with the heap of sawdust that had been soaked in gasoline, was slowly creeping down a trail of wood shavings on one side of the trailer. The flames rose high, licking at me and the horse's flanks.

Carefully, I crossed in front of the horse, avoiding a quick stomp.

I dragged the toolbox as far away from the fire as I could and opened it. Inside were two brick-sized bars of something squishy wrapped in waxed paper. The covering said "Semtex." I ripped it off. Inside was gray stuff that looked like Silly Putty.

"This has got to be some of the missing plastic explosives," I said. "Do you think there's enough to blast open the side of the trailer?"

"Do the door instead," she said. "Blast off the door handle or the hinges."

I took one of the bricks of plastic and tore off a blob. I pressed it all around the doorknob, hoping to blow off the outside metal latch so we could kick the door open. I picked up a long wood chip that was lit on the edge, using it like a match. I touched the plastic with the flame. I held it for about five seconds. When the wood was about to singe my fingers, I dropped it. The plastic was on fire.

"Duck!" I yelled.

We huddled against the side of the trailer as far away from the door as Thunderbolt would let us. I could barely see because the smoke from the burning sawdust was rising, bringing tears.

"The plastic is burning," said Jade in between coughs. "Why won't it explode?"

"Stay low," I said. "There's more air near the bottom. I'm going to try again."

There were a few weird things in the bottom of the toolbox. They had a white button in the center. I remembered that when Ms. Haveshire dressed as a crew member with a mustache, she needed wire to make the bombs explode.

Taking out another lump of clay, I rolled it into a long snake as I'd seen people do in the movies. I pressed the long snake around the door frame, careful to stay away from the burning doorknob. "Do you think that's enough?" I asked Jade. When I got no answer, I turned. Jade lay slumped against the wall, unconscious. Thunderbolt was still dancing, trying to stay away from the fire. He bumped the latch and his gate swung open. He was free to trample my sister.

I can't stop to help her. It may only be seconds before all the air is gone.

I pushed one of the weird clumps of wire into the

plastic. Then I pushed the button and jumped back immediately. I dragged Jade back a bit and then lay on top of her, covering her body with mine.

The boom was louder than a cannon. There was no fire; instead a white light flashed and left a cloud of smoke. Around the door frame where the Semtex had been, light pierced through. I was going to kick in the door, but Thunderbolt beat me to it with one quick thrust of his back hoof. He was the first one out of the trailer.

Twenty-seven

The ambulance crew wouldn't let me off the gurney when I got to the hospital. Both Jade and I were hooked up to oxygen masks and had thick black belts holding us down. The emergency room admitting nurse was the same one who had been on duty when Jade had come in for her burn. She said, "Hey, why don't you girls take up alligator wrestling? It's a lot safer."

Jade had enough energy to laugh underneath the mask. It took me a while to figure out the joke. I was out of it. My head ached more than when I first woke up after Jade slammed the gate into me. Without a fire to worry about, I had plenty of time to think about the pain in my temple. It was so bad, I couldn't focus my eyes. I pretty much kept them shut, so I didn't see what was going on.

Of all the people who came from the studio to the hospital, Mrs. Kennett was the only one who was allowed into the examination rooms. While I was waiting for tests, she told us what had happened. At lunchtime, she noticed us missing and started asking questions, which caused a big ruckus. She insisted Mr. Knighton stop production and begin a search. At first, he waved her away, saying it was LaShondra's job. But

the security guard agreed with Mrs. Kennett. Even though Marcus had been arrested, the bombing was still fresh in everyone's mind. The crew was in a mood to be paranoid.

But it was Chantella who took charge. As soon as she arrived and heard the news she brought an AD's bullhorn to the caterer's silver truck and demanded that everyone in the lunch line look for us. Knighton couldn't do much to stop her. No one complained; they all milled around and began to search. Snap figured that we'd be near the horse since he'd heard Jade talking about it. He was the first person I saw when I stumbled out of the trailer, dragging an unconscious Jade.

"Snap," I said, angry and exhausted, "if you say trying to burn someone up inside a horse trailer isn't evil—you're crazy."

"I'll take your word for it," he said, rushing to help me carry Jade.

I remember staring into his eyes, which were dark and bright with excitement, and then collapsing, the asphalt hot and sticky next to my cheek.

Mrs. Kennett told me some more of the details. She said Sergio—Thunderbolt's groom—was being questioned by the police when she left to follow the ambulance. He was suspected since he was in charge of the trailer, and the explosives had been inside.

I don't remember much about the X-rays except a doctor in murky green scrub clothes said that if the gate had hit even three quarters of an inch forward, I would have been killed. Later, I endured the paper dress, the needles, and going to the bathroom with a nurse watching over me to make sure I didn't faint. The doctor gave me a pretty good pain reliever and a bed, and as soon as everyone was done poking me, I fell asleep.

*****

When I woke up hours later, I found out that I did have friends. Several cards were waiting on the nightstand next to my bed. Tasha and Ryan had dropped off a card signed by them and three other girls from school. They also brought the world's largest chocolate chip cookie. There was the same bouquet of flowers from Galaxy Studios as had been sent to Jade. And a crystal necklace. I left mine draped round the stem of a flower.

My first visitor was the pastor. Thank goodness Jade was in the room. She had wandered down the hall without permission, just to make sure I was OK. The pastor came in wearing the tombstone tie.

"Well, how are you, Shadrach and Abednego?" he asked. "Where's Meshach?"

We looked at him as if he were speaking a foreign language. "Oh," he continued, seeing our confused faces, "that's a Bible story about three men who got thrown in a furnace because they wouldn't worship a golden statue."

I thought he was going to bore us with some long history lesson. I'd been reading in the Books of Chronicles, and parts of them were just long lists of people. I wasn't too thrilled to hear about those guys with weird names. But Jade asked, "What's wrong with a beautiful statue? God is part of everything, and so worshiping the statue is like worshiping Him."

"Well, those three men didn't think so. They knew there is a difference between God and what He has created or what man has created. So they told the king they wouldn't worship the statue, even if it meant death."

"What happened?" I asked, interested now.

"God saved them," he said. I could tell he was trying to tell the story simply, so we wouldn't be confused. "In fact, an angel was inside with them. When the king looked into the furnace, he saw *four* men. And when the three came out, they weren't burned, and they didn't even smell like smoke."

My sister began to cry. Jade always did overreact. When we were seven, we stole fake jewelry from a local drugstore. When Dad found out, he made us go back to pay for the plastic rings and bracelet. Jade brought her entire savings and her favorite stuffed animal, a long-haired cat with bright emerald-green eyes. It was so filthy from being dragged around that its fur was matted with clumps of pudding, dirt, and strawberry punch. She made the store manager keep the money and the cat. When he tried to give the toy back, she burst into tears. Just like now.

She lay facedown on the foot of my bed in a thin, hospital-issue, blue cotton robe. She sobbed harder than she had the day of the first fire. I had wanted her to change her mind, but this was more than I expected.

The pastor wasn't too comfortable with what he'd started. "Oh, goodness." He looked as if he wanted to comfort her. He lifted his hand to put it on her head. But then he stopped himself.

"Maybe it was a miracle today," I said. "And God sent me to help you. You were in there all alone at first."

"*You* got us out," Jade said. "With a bomb, not God."

"But God made sure the Semtex was there," I answered. "I had no idea that Sergio had hidden it there."

"Jade," the pastor said, "if you want to, you can refuse to see the good that God does. You can say it comes

from somewhere else—nature, other people, inside yourself. I know a lot of people who won't admit that God does good things. But they sure do blame Him when things get tough."

"What's wrong with that?" Jade asked. "What's the use of believing in God if He won't spare you from trouble?"

"Look," said the pastor, his voice gentle but also no-nonsense, "God didn't save Jesus from dying on the cross. Jesus suffered, and so did His followers. God promises *spiritual* peace, not safety and happiness. Before those three men went into the furnace, they had no idea if God was going to save them. In fact, they told the king that their God could save them, but even if He didn't, they would never worship the statue. Those men knew that God *could* protect them, but He *might* not."

"Then God must hate me," Jade said, "because I'm so mad at Him for letting me get burned. Then He kicked me out of the movie." Jade cried more, her eyes turning an ugly shade of strawberry.

"No," I said, "Mr. Knighton kicked you out, and Ms. Haveshire probably put the pyro fluid in the makeup room; she burned you." But Jade didn't stop crying much. "Please," I said, beginning to cry myself, "just don't say God hates you. He doesn't hate anyone."

All Jade did was cry. I didn't feel too bad that I couldn't change her mind. The pastor didn't either, and he knew more than I did. He left us some brochures on the bedside. He said good-bye. It wasn't till then that I realized that the pattern on his tie had actually been little crosses inside of arched windows. Not tombstones as a sign of death, but an empty cross, a sign of life.

Twenty-eight

Dad came, finally. It took him so long to get there because he had been performing surgery. "I hope the woman's chin is evenly tucked in," he joked. "I heard the news right after I had made the incision. I had to suture it up before I left, so I went ahead and finished the facelift. But I was distracted thinking about you two."

Jade was in my room sitting in a wheelchair. She got to be discharged, now that Dad was there, but I had to stay overnight for observation. The X-rays showed a concussion, and no one wanted to let me out in case my brain swelled or clotted up or whatever brains do when they've been bashed about.

"Did you two hear about Thunderbolt?" Dad asked.

We shook our heads.

"Mrs. Kennett called me on the cell phone," he said, "and said that a vet just put him down."

I saw tears welling up in Jade's eyes again. We both knew that "put him down" meant he was dead.

"Don't worry," Dad continued. "With that kind of shot, the horse's brain dies in about a minute. There's no pain."

I always wondered how people knew that. I wanted

to say, "How do you know?" Adults say the same thing about dogs and cats that never leave the animal shelters alive. But I hoped for Thunderbolt's sake it was true.

"Why?" I did ask. "He was fine once he got out of the trailer."

"He bolted," Jade said. "Snap told me he saw him fall over a bicycle. It was as if he didn't even see it. But he only went down to his knees."

"He was a thoroughbred, all right," said Dad. "Their legs are like uncooked spaghetti. It doesn't take much to snap 'em in half."

"What will they do for the movie?" Jade asked, crying in earnest again. But this time, it wasn't sobs. Just quiet weeping, as if she were cutting open an onion.

"A horse is a horse, I guess," Dad said. "He'll be easier to replace than you two will be."

"Replace us?" I said. "Why doesn't Mr. Knighton want me? I'm physically fine, and I was doing great." I didn't mention Jade's run-in with the director yet. I wanted her to tell Dad herself.

"It's not Knighton," my father said. "I took you out of the film." He looked me straight in the eye. "This is the second time one of you has landed in the hospital. Yesterday was a near miss. I won't have it. I've already contacted the SAG lawyers. They say we have every right to walk out. The primary responsibility of the film company is to make sure there is a safe working environment. In fact, when I called SAG, I found out there's a special hot line to notify if you think a set is dangerous. I think a fire, bombings, and being maliciously trapped in a burning horse trailer count as being dangerous."

"But—" I tried to argue.

"I refuse to discuss this, McKenna." He turned to

Jade. "Let's go check you out." He turned back to me, trying to be cheerful after dropping an information bomb that made yesterday's seem small. "We'll be back first thing tomorrow, honey. Try to sleep. Be sure you take the pain medication. That's some wallop you got there."

I saw the river of tears streaming down Jade's face as Dad wheeled her out of the room. As soon as the door closed, my own stream washed over my face.

*****

The bouquet from Mr. Neverland was more of an apology than a get-well wish. It was a rainbow of strange tropical flowers. When he carried it in the next morning, I couldn't tell who carried it because the flowers spanned the whole doorway and covered his face.

"I've got good news and bad news," he said.

"What's the good news, Mr. Neverland?" I asked, recognizing his voice. After not being able to finish the movie, I couldn't handle any more bad news.

"Marcus will give evidence against his mother," he said, putting the flowers on the window ledge. "It was she who was doing it all along. At first, Marcus confessed to protect her."

I held back all the I-told-you-sos and simply asked, "What's going to happen to him?"

"He'll get some sentence for obstructing justice and all, but I don't think he knew she was doing it until he found her with some Semtex on the day of the explosions."

"But why did she do it?" I asked. "Is she some sort of pyromaniac who loves to watch things burn?"

"No." He was still rearranging the flowers on the win-

dow ledge, his back toward me. "I still think I was right that it was someone looking for attention—someone looking for attention for her son. She wanted him to be famous. She couldn't stand it that her son was only a firefighter, not a movie star. She set the fires so Marcus could put them out and become a hero—maybe even have his own program on network TV."

Poor Marcus.

The investigator turned around. "I'm sorry for not listening to you when you said you saw someone else setting the bombs. I guess I was trying to be a hero too. I was so proud of myself for catching Marcus and getting a confession. . . ." Mr. Neverland was standing too far away for me to see his eyes, but he was sniffling. I'll bet that at least one drop of water was rolling down his cheek, even if there wasn't a river. Or maybe the plants were giving him hay fever.

"That's OK," I said. "I should have told you about the toolbox. I wanted to give it to another officer so that you would be sorry for not listening to me."

Both of us were silent. I was thinking how close I'd come to dying because I let myself get angry. He was probably thinking he'd come close to letting an arsonist kill two people because he thought he knew it all.

"OK. What's the bad news?" I broke the weird silence.

"Ms. Haveshire's gone," he said in his raspy voice. "The guard remembers her leaving the studio back lot before he heard the trailer door blast open. He said she smiled and waved. We tried to track her yesterday, but I think she made it out of the country."

"Will someone follow her?"

"They're trying. But you've got to remember, McKenna, she's been in the film industry a long time.

143

You didn't recognize her when she dressed up as a set carpenter, and you saw her at close range."

I thought about the little gardener, who had really been Ms. Haveshire in costume. The mustache might have given her the rash above her lip.

"Her bank records show that she probably had a lot of cash stored up," he continued, "not to mention two or three false passports. I've learned that celebrities use those a lot to get around without the press finding them."

"So, somewhere in this world, a woman who wants me dead is roaming free." It was hard to look on the bright side.

"I think if she meant to kill you, she would have. She certainly knew enough about special effects and about chemicals. She'd been helping Marcus study for his arson investigator exams. And she had worked on many films with special effects. She knew how to get at Al's stuff. She put down on his call sheet that he was going to have to blow up more horse stables. So he brought more explosives the other day. All he really needed was some oil to make smoke. So he was loaded with the stuff when she broke into his equipment."

"Why didn't he lock it up better?"

"He followed regulations. The assistants are trained and took every precaution. Haveshire just got to it; we haven't figured out how, yet."

"What about the fire in the trailer?"

"Well, we didn't find much residue of gasoline. Maybe she threw her cigarette in just to give you a scare."

"Well, I smelled it, and she did say she was trying to kill me. But I suppose that doesn't count for much. What do I know?"

Mr. Neverland laughed. "I still don't seem to want to listen much to you, do I? OK, you win. She was trying to kill you."

For some reason winning the point didn't comfort me much.

Twenty-nine

It wasn't until a week later, after I was back in school, a green-eyed brunette, and just a normal student again, that I remembered Ashley Saunders.

I was at my locker, spinning the combination lock, when someone came up from behind me and covered my eyes with his fingers. "Who is it?" I asked.

"You know who," said Tasha's voice.

You know who! That was the signature on Ashley's note. I never did find out who sent it.

"Tasha, that may be your voice, but these are Ryan's hands or you need a manicure something awful."

When he released his hands, I turned and saw Tasha standing with him. She spoke first. "Ryan and I are going to be extras on the set of *Thoroughbred Fever* tomorrow. They need teenagers for a mall crowd scene. Jade says your dad won't let you back on the set. But . . . I thought you could at least ask him if you could come too."

I knew I wouldn't go back as an extra, even if Dad drove me himself. It would be like tasting double chocolate fudge ice cream and then settling for sawdust. Being a principal actor with a wardrobe, a dressing room, and more than sixty lines in a major motion pic-

ture, and then being an extra who wouldn't even get near Chantella or Knighton—that was too big a drop for me. I might even have to watch whoever it was who got Cassidy's role. *Could there be anything more painful?*

"I don't want to go, Tash," I said.

Ryan said, "See, I told you it was a dumb idea."

I didn't want them feeling bad for me. That was my own job. I thought of something to cheer them up. "But I'd like you guys to come with us to the premiere of *Clone Colony.*"

"Oh my gosh!" Tash said. She started jumping up and down. I thought her large, dangling earrings would rip out of her earlobes—they were flopping so hard with her bouncing. "What will I wear? Oh, I've got to find Jade! We've got to go shopping." She started to run, her high heels clicking loudly on the red tile. She stopped and turned. "Thanks, McKenna," she said, and ran again. I hoped she wouldn't be like Thunderbolt and break one of her toothpick-thin legs as she rushed down the hallway.

"I don't have to wear a dress, do I?" asked Ryan.

"Only if you shave your legs," I said, nervous. I hadn't talked to him since I'd gotten back to school. I didn't like telling about having to quit. It hurt too much.

"You know," said Ryan, "that was nice of you to invite Tash, even after she put your phone number on the internet."

"Don't forget the picture of the rat."

"OK. And the rat," he laughed.

"She'll never admit it," I said.

"Well, she told me, and she's really sorry. You know, she was in the office the other day when the phone rang. The secretary was out of the office, and she answered it."

"So?" I started to walk down the hall to my next class. I didn't want Ryan knowing I'd gladly be tardy to keep talking to him. He was wearing a black shirt and black jeans. It made his hair look dark and his eyes even more forest green than normal.

"So," he said, following me, "it was the new casting director for *Thoroughbred Fever*, looking for someone to play Cassidy."

My heart stopped. *If someone from this school gets that job, I'll move to Siberia.* "What did she say? Did she volunteer to audition herself?"

"No," he said, "she told him there was no one else here with your talent and experience."

"You're making this up," I started to walk faster. The whole conversation was churning up my very soul. "It never happened. Tasha wouldn't say that about me. Jade maybe. But not me."

"No way," he said, "I know because I was in the office. I heard her use your name."

"So no one from this school is getting the part, or even auditioning?"

"Not if Tasha can help it."

I needed to mull that over in my mind. Tasha and I might be friends yet. But I didn't want to think about it then, so I changed the subject.

"Why were you in the office?" I asked. For this question, I stopped walking.

"I had to go before the school board and tell them about the chemistry room fire."

"Are you off the hook?"

"Yes and no. I have several hours of community service to perform, but no criminal charges will be pressed. And I won't be kicked out unless I get sent to Mr. Harley's office again."

The class bell rang.

"Well," I said, straightening my books, "I gotta go to class."

But Ryan was already gone, sprinting down the hall. It was going to be hard for him to keep away from Mr. Harley if he was always tardy.

Thirty

Jade talked Dad into renting a limousine to take us to the crew and cast showing of *Clone Colony*. We wanted a white or pink one, but Dad settled on a plain black Cadillac. That night, all five of us got out of the long dark car in front of the Galaxy Studios Theater, which was on the studio grounds.

Tasha was overwhelmed because of all the stars and other powerful Hollywood people who were there. Jade whispered, "Tash, you can't ask for autographs here, OK?" Tash nodded, barely listening.

Dad was wearing the tuxedo he had worn for his and Mom's wedding. I didn't know whether to be proud that he wasn't fat like a lot of dads and could still wear it or be embarrassed because it was so out of fashion. I wished he at least would have gotten a shirt without ruffles. All the other men in tuxedos had shirts with pleats, not ruffles. But maybe that was too much to ask for. Dad hated shopping, for himself or anyone else.

Not Tasha. She bought six dresses for the occasion, planning on returning the five she didn't wear. The one she chose was green and black with sequins all over. She looked ready to win an Oscar. Jade and I dressed alike. The dresses had a fitted white top with spaghetti

straps, and a black skirt that came down just above the knee. Only the tip-top of Jade's gauze bandage could be seen. We had on black shoes with a low heel, while Tasha's heels were as pointed as an ice pick.

The showing was supposed to be for the cast. But so many people were there that hadn't worked on the movie, I felt as if we were at the wrong place. But Jade did spot Mr. Romano, the director, almost right away. Ryan elbowed me when she pointed him out. "See," he hissed in a whisper, "I'm not the only one wearing jeans."

"I was so, so sorry," Mr. Romano said, after greeting us by flashing his gold tooth in a smile, "to hear about *Thoroughbred Fever*. I know Knighton was sick to lose you, but everyone understands. The trouble on that set was worse than the problems we had on *Colony*."

Next he shook Dad's and Ryan's hands, smiled at Tasha, kissed Jade's and my cheeks, and left to hobnob with the other movie moguls.

I didn't think Jade and I or Ryan or Tash could drink the champagne chilling in ice buckets. Dad seldom drank alcohol, except for beer now and then, but that night he got a glass of champagne. When Tasha took a tall, thin glass, Dad didn't say anything, but Ryan did. "Tash," he almost growled, "put that down."

"I can't. Someone else might pick it up, and I've already got my germs on it." She'd also gotten lipstick round the rim. "Besides, my parents won't care."

"But Dr. James will. Knock it off." Ryan's whole face scowled, even his eyebrows. Tasha gave him a look that said mind your own business, swallowed the whole glass, and put it down. A waiter came by and scooped it up.

I rolled my eyes.

But that was mostly it. We just stood around, commenting on people's clothes, and waited to be let in to the theater. There were a few reporters. One asked Jade about the latest fire in the trailer, but that was old news by now.

I didn't see Chantella until we were sitting down. She was there, dangling on the arm of a very tall, bald man. They sat four rows ahead of us. Mr. Romano spoke some kind words to the audience before the film rolled.

Jade performed sweet as anything and was in a lot more scenes than I had been in, even though I had more lines. Seeing myself on the big screen for the first time was weird. I'd never noticed how wide movie screens are. In one or two close-ups, my nose looked as big as a car. I thought I'd like to do some scenes over, but it was too late. All my mistakes were forever captured on celluloid. Millions of people would see them. I couldn't keep them a secret. I just had to smile and do better next time. If there was ever a next time.

Instead of making me happy, seeing the movie made me feel heavy, as if I'd eaten an entire large pizza and a pan of brownies all by myself. I wanted to keep doing movies, and I felt as though the door had been closed. I was glad to have Ryan and Tash there. They could understand; their careers hadn't gone very far either.

So when we got out into the red-and-gold lobby, I was pretty much depressed. I wanted to crawl into bed and hope the sun would never come up. But Dad was already talking to someone about the new eye-tuck technique for people who had already had plastic surgery. Jade and Tasha had found "Jake" Jacobs, a friend from the *Clone Colony* cast who had once been an actor. She and Jade were already laughing.

All of sudden, Ryan grabbed my arm. "McKenna," he

said in an excited tone, but not loud. "Look, there she is."

Through the glass door, I caught a glimpse of a blond head walking past the theater. Not even hesitating a second, I ran to catch up with her, my shoes tip-tapping on the concrete. "Ashley!" I called.

She turned and sneered when she saw me. "Hello. What do you want? Such a big star talking to a lowly soap worker, it must be important."

"Just wondered how you were," I said, trying hard to be nice. I needed information from her, and getting in a fight would get me nowhere.

"I'm fine. I just got done with work on *Seems Like Eternity*," she said. "They're going to increase my character's role with more lines. I still have connections, you know."

"What connections did you have with Ms. Haveshire?" I asked. We were walking side by side, heading to the parking lot. "Seems as if you two were awfully tight for a while."

"What do you mean by that?" Her eyes narrowed.

"Well, there's the fact that she gave you the part . . . and passed you secret notes."

I knew by the look on her face that I was on to something. She didn't answer, just walked quickly and stiffly to her car. Her shiny curls shimmered as the light from the streetlights bathed them. She stopped at a red sports car. As she fiddled with her keys, I asked, "Did you know that Ms. Haveshire set the fire on the set of that commercial you were in?"

Whatever she knew had to come out. She was too much of a braggart not to tell. She thought I was stupid and had to let me know it.

"I had her figured out the day she did it. The rest of you were fools, including that Investigator Neverland."

"Then why didn't you turn her in? Stop her before she hurt someone?"

"Well," she said and smiled with false innocence, "why would I do that? There was nothing in it for me."

"OK. I get it. You found out she did the first fire, then you blackmailed her into giving you the Cassidy part."

She laughed a high, screechy squeal. "You can't prove it."

"Then Haveshire went after *you*. Don't bother to deny it. I have the note asking you to meet her in your dressing room. That wasn't such a smart move."

"Well, I got out of the fire in time, didn't I? And it's going to make a nice lawsuit against Galaxy Studios. I'll be rich when this is over. You should do the same."

"You'll be lucky to keep your soap opera part," I said. "People who turn their back on Hollywood are shunned for life. Winning a lawsuit will get you money, but your reputation as a troublemaker will ruin you."

I admired her nose as she stuck it in the air. Dad had done a good job. He didn't deserve to be sued just because she was in a fire and said her nasal passages didn't work. Just because she was greedy.

She turned away from me and got in the car. As the engine started, I couldn't help one last comment. "You only used the fire as an excuse to get off the set," I yelled so she could hear it above the roar of the engine. "Knighton was going to fire you!"

As the car moved forward out of the space, she rolled down the window to yell something back. But her words were lost when, from out of nowhere, there was a heavy thud and a blur of blue and black flashed over her hood.

Ryan!

"You hit me!" he yelled. He lay on his back in the parking lot, reaching for his neck. "I'm gonna sue you!"

Ashley got out of the car. "You saw him, McKenna! He jumped in front of me." Her voice, now that she wanted something, was smooth as satin underwear, and just as feminine.

"I didn't see anything," I said, which was true. I had been too focused on listening to what she was going to yell.

"I'm gonna sue you," Ryan moaned again. Both of his hands were behind his neck. "Oh, the pain. The *pain!*"

"Look," Ashley said, "if you don't report this, I'll . . . I'll give you ten thousand dollars."

"Cash?" Ryan asked.

"Cash," Ashley said firmly.

"No deal," Ryan said. "I'm sure it's whiplash. I'll have problems the rest of my life. My acting career is over."

"Twenty thousand," Ashley said. Her voice was beginning to warble.

"No," Ryan moaned.

"What, then?" she begged. "How much?"

"No cash," he said. "Just drop the lawsuit against Dr. James. Then I think my neck would feel a lot better."

Ashley looked as if she wanted to spit on him. Any beauty she had was gone, twisted away in a grimace of hatred. "All right. I'll drop it." She climbed back in the red car, making sure her dress hem didn't get caught in the door when she slammed it. Out of the window, she said, "Get out of the way."

Ryan had only a second or two to roll out of the way. The tires squealed as her car tore out of the parking lot, barely missing a couple of people walking our way.

Thirty-one

"Get up, Ryan," I said. "Are you OK?"

But he was shaking too hard from laughter to stand. I reached down to help him get up, and he pulled me down with him. I started to laugh too.

That's how Chantella and the bald man found us— sitting in the parking lot underneath a streetlight, cracking up so hard, we couldn't even speak without gasping for air. I was laughing away all the disappointment and fear of the last few weeks. I felt free. I had finally figured out how Ashley and Ms. Haveshire were connected. And with Ryan's help, I had won a small victory. Ashley wasn't going to sue my dad.

"McKenna?" Chantella said. "Are you OK? We saw Ashley almost run you and your friend down." I nodded, still laughing. But I stopped when Chantella introduced the bald man.

"Cain," she said, "this is McKenna, the girl I told you about. One of the clones in the movie we just saw." I struggled to stand up. It wasn't easy, because I was trying to keep my dress from creeping up. I had to use one hand to hold down my hem. Offering his hand, the man helped me up. His hand was warm and strong. Chantella continued the introduction. "McKenna, this is

Cain Snyder." I shook the hand I was already holding.

At the name, Ryan stood straight up and brushed off his hands on the seat of his jeans. "I'm Ryan Kennett, sir." He offered his newly cleaned palm. "Pleased to meet you."

By the formality in Ryan's voice, I guessed he knew Cain Snyder was someone very important. And if beautiful Chantella was dating him, he had to have something going for him, like brains, power, or money. Perhaps all three.

"Hi," I said. "I hope you liked the movie."

"I did," he said. "In fact, I'd like for you to audition for a role in a movie. The working title is *A Rope and Some Courage*. It's based on the life of a real cowgirl and trick rider. Chantella is taking the lead role, but we need someone to play her as a young cowgirl just learning to ride."

I looked at Chantella, who appeared unlike a cowgirl in a clinging, black dress. She nodded her approval, giving me a smile. Since Cain had seen the movie, I felt better about agreeing. I didn't want any favors from Chantella. I only wanted to get a job because I was good.

"But what about my sister?" I asked. "Can she audition, too?"

A pause in his response and the quick look he gave Chantella told me they'd talked about that possibility before. Chantella answered for him. "Of course she can read for the part, McKenna. But I never worked with her. I can only give Cain the recommendation that you've got enough spunk to carry it off. And, if you both read, only one is getting the part. We don't need two cowgirls."

I nodded.

"But," Cain said, "I saw this young man take a great roll over that red car. Why don't you keep in touch. We'll be hiring the supporting cast after the principals are chosen. We need a few young rodeo clowns."

Ryan was ready. "Sure," he said, reaching into his pocket. "Here's my card. My agent's number is at the bottom."

*****

In the limousine on the way home, Dad leaned his head back and said, "I shouldn't have had that second glass of champagne. It always gives me a splitting headache." He closed his eyes and tuned us out.

Tasha and I were riding in the seat directly behind the driver, facing backward; Jade and Ryan sat across from us. There was a minibar inside the limo, tiny button lights all around the ceiling and floor, and incredibly soft, white leather seats.

Tasha began to tell us all about the famous people she had met while Ryan and I had been outside. "Too bad," she said, "Jade and I got to meet Lincoln Anderson, the hottest action-adventure movie star. He thought I was twenty."

Jade said, "It was really no big deal." She never had been one for bragging.

Ryan, however, was different. "Well, McKenna and I," he said, "got offered parts in a new movie."

"Sure," Tasha said, "I suppose a producer came up to you and said, 'What a face! I'm gonna make you a star!' " I gently kicked Ryan's foot. When he looked up, I shook my head to get him not to tell the story. I wanted to tell Jade about Cain Snyder and the audition in private. I didn't want her thinking God hated her just because

Chantella put in a good word for me.

Ryan picked up on my cue, and when neither he nor I responded to Tasha's taunting, she giggled. "Well Lincoln Anderson said Jade had been fabulous in *Clone Colony.* What if you get a role in a movie with him, Jade? What if you have to kiss him? Would a first kiss be a big deal then? Or wouldn't it count 'cause it's in a movie?"

"Well, since she's already been kissed by Snap Herez, I guess she'd get used to it." I said, and then regretted it, because I saw the look on Jade's face. It was flushed as red as Tasha's fingernail polish.

"What? When did that happen?" Tasha demanded.

"It was nothing," Jade said. "After the fire in the trailer, Snap was the first person to find us. He had to give me mouth-to-mouth, because I wasn't breathing. I don't even remember it."

"Oh my gosh," Tasha said. "Your first kiss. By Snap Herez. . . .Would you ever go out with him?"

I almost spoke up to defend Jade, but she managed to pipe up first. "It wasn't a first kiss," she said. "It doesn't count if the guy has to do it for mouth-to-mouth." She smiled at me, both of us remembering the conversation we'd had about kisses in the school office. "Plus," she went on, "Dad won't let us date. And besides, Snap is into the New Age, and after reading about it some, I don't think God would like it if I got into that stuff."

I just about fell off the seat. I looked at Jade's neck. No pointed crystal hung there. And her bracelet with the words "Daughter of God" was back on her wrist. When she smiled at me, I knew I had my twin sister back.

LIGHTS, CAMERA, ACTION! MYSTERIES

Trouble Shooting

Smoke Screen Secret

Rodeo Rough Cut

Book 2